Holding On

There was a trolley ahead of them, and Veronica motioned with her head as her skates began gathering speed. The trolley stopped, people got off and on, and breathlessly, they reached it just as it began moving again. Veronica held on to the back of the trolley with one hand and continued holding her candy with the other. But Peter let his drop, as he held on with both hands.

The trolley jerked to a start and yanked them along over the cobblestone streets, faster, faster, faster.

Other Apple Paperbacks
by Marilyn Sachs:

Peter and Veronica

Peter and Veronica

Marilyn Sachs

illustrated by
Louis Glanzman

AN
APPLE
PAPERBACK

SCHOLASTIC INC.
New York Toronto London Auckland Sydney

Grateful acknowledgments are due Rabbi Bernard W. Kimmel of the Beth Shalom Synagogue in San Francisco for reading the bar mitzvah chapter, and offering his advice.

ISBN 0-590-40404-0

12 11 10 9 8 7 6 5 4 3   7 8 9/8 0 1 2/9

Printed in the U.S.A.   28

First Scholastic printing, April 1987

For my nephews, Steven, Dan, Chris, and Arthur,
who wanted a book about a boy.

Peter and Veronica

1

Friday afternoon. No Hebrew School. He could do what he liked today. Peter dropped his books on his bed, grabbed his roller skates, and was out of the house before his mother could ask him where he was going.

Outside, he sat down on the stoop, quickly strapped on his skates, and skimmed off down the street. Funny how he hadn't skated for years until a few weeks ago. Whether it was his friend who had decided to start skating again or whether it was his idea, he couldn't actually remember. But now the two of them skated almost any free afternoon they had, which wasn't much these days what with *cheder* every day after school except Friday.

Peter zipped around the corner at Boston Road and began picking up speed.

"Hey, Peter! Wait up, Peter!" somebody shouted. Reluctantly Peter allowed his skates to decelerate and looked behind him. "Oh hi, Marv," he said, as Marvin Green lumbered up to him, dragging a long piece of galvanized pipe behind him. "Whatcha got?"

Marv's face was rapturous. "Look," he said, "it's got a valve on it—and it was lying right out on the lot next to the grocery store."

"Mmm," Peter said approvingly.

"Where are you going now?" Marv asked. "Do you want to come home with me and work on the shack?"

"I can't," said Peter. "I'm going skating with another friend. How about Sunday? You going to be working on it Sunday?"

"I guess so."

"Good! I'll see you then."

Marv patted the pipe lovingly and said, "Don't come too early. My father has to sleep."

"O.K., I'll be there about nine." He nodded to Marv and began moving off. A short thrust with his right foot, a long swoop with his left, and the wind came stronger and stronger in his face as he zoomed along. He had to slow down to cross the street, but on the block where his friend lived, he went whizzing along down to the last house on the corner.

Nobody on the stoop, so he climbed up the steps on his skates, holding his arms out on either side of him. He didn't even have to hold on any more. Into the vestibule he clattered and rang the bell marked R. PETRONSKI—4D with their prearranged signal,

"DA DA-DA-DA DA . . ." And in a second came the answering buzz, "DUM, DUM."

Peter moved outside on the stoop to wait. After a few minutes he became impatient, and was just going to go back inside the vestibule and ring the bell again, when he heard a window opening overhead. He looked up and saw it was the right window, three stories above his head.

"What's keeping you?" he shouted.

A small hand holding a paper bag emerged from the window. The bag dropped. Peter lurched to the other side of the stoop and the bag whizzed by his head, plopped on the ground, ripped open, and a geyser of water erupted from its insides.

There was the sound of a happy laugh, then a howl, then the window being banged closed.

Peter inched nervously around the remains of the bag, hurried down the stairs (holding on), and stood waiting uncertainly by the curb. After a few more minutes, the vestibule door opened and Peter's friend came hurrying out.

"That rotten kid," she said. "He's jealous."

"Hi, Veronica," Peter said. "Was that Stanley?"

"Who else?" said Veronica, her eyes narrowing. "I fixed him though, but let's go before he comes after me. It won't hurt him to stay with Mary Rose for a change. Come on, hurry up!"

Veronica, holding her skates, began running down the block and Peter skated quickly behind her. They both could hear the window opening again, and a voice full of anguish cry, "Veronica, Veronica! Take me too! Veronica, Veronica . . ."

Peter could see Veronica's shoulders quivering but she ran faster, and he skated faster, around the corner, across the street, down another block, around another corner, until the tormented voice could no longer be heard.

"Phew!" Peter gasped when they finally stopped. "What a pest that kid is!"

Veronica's chest was heaving, and she sat down on the curb and laid her skates down at her side.

"He keeps sticking his tongue out at me," Peter complained, "and last week he threw a banana at me. What did I ever do to him?"

Veronica began strapping her skates on. "Never mind that," she said. "You don't have to live with him."

"I'd kill myself if I did," said Peter.

Veronica finished with one foot and began strapping on the other skate.

"Every time he sees me he says, 'Yah, Yah, Yah' to me. What's biting him? And why doesn't he wipe his nose?"

"Listen," Veronica shouted, looking up at him, her eyes blazing, "you leave him alone. He's only five, and . . . you just . . . don't make fun of him."

"Are you crazy?" Peter yelled back. "Whose side are you on, anyway?"

Veronica shrugged her shoulders, finished strapping on her skate, and stood up. She was at least a head taller than Peter, and for a minute the two of them stood looking at each other, waiting. Then Veronica smiled. "Let's go," she said.

And that was that. One thing about Veronica, Peter reflected as the two of them whizzed off down the street in the direction of the big outdoor market place that lay at the bottom of the hill, you never had to waste time talking about where you were going or what you were going to do—you just went and did. Right now, for instance, there were any number of places they might have considered. They could have turned left and headed for the park, or right and whizzed down the broad, flat steppes of Prospect Avenue, or even back toward Boston Road and into the hill country. But somehow, without any discussion, here were the two of them, completely in accord, flying down Jennings Street to the market.

Veronica moved out in front. With her long legs she generally took the lead, disappearing from time to time but always reappearing at critical moments. Right now there was something lying on the ground in front of her, and Peter saw her body move into a crouch as she held out her arms and jumped cleanly over the obstruction. He braced himself, knowing that as good a skater as he might be, he was still not in the same league as Veronica. The obstruction turned out to be a child's truck, and he concentrated on it nervously as he zoomed closer. Now! Peter flexed his muscles, held out his arms, leaped, and landed safely upright. A little wobbly, perhaps, but he'd done it.

Ahead of him, he saw Veronica race toward two girls walking together, laughed as he watched them spring apart, and called out, "Hi, Reba, Hi, Edna," as he followed in the path Veronica had blazed for him between the two of them.

"You crazy or something, Peter Wedemeyer!" Edna shouted, and Reba began giggling. Reba had a way of giggling lately whenever she saw him with Veronica that irritated him, and he began wobbling. Muttering under his breath about fat girls who giggled, he held out both arms to steady himself, and kept his eyes on Veronica. The hill grew steep now, and he felt his knees quivering, while ahead of him Veronica nervelessly sailed down on one leg.

Down at the bottom finally, he looked around for her. There were so many people, mostly women with shopping bags and young children. Across from where he was standing lay the market place with all its outdoor stands and its mingled aromas of pickles, bread, smoked fish, and honey. He sniffed the air hungrily, as he always did down here, and fingered the empty pockets of his jacket.

"Hey, Peter! Here, Peter!" Veronica yelled. She had already crossed the street and was beckoning to him from the other side. He skated toward her, moving through the crowd of shoppers.

"You have any money?" she asked.

"No! You?"

"No."

Slowly they skated along the street, stopping to salivate over trays of halvah, sesame candies, nuts, pickles, and all the fragrant dainties that lay on top of the numerous stands. The peddlers' voices mingled with their cries of "Three for a nickel," "Two for a penny," "Fresh . . . fresh . . . fresh," and the answering retorts of the shoppers, "I won't give you a penny over a nickel," or "You crook, you, the nuts are all rotten!"

Peter was dreamily sniffing the air over a barrel of sour pickles when Veronica pressed something into his hand. It was a strip of shoe-leather candy, and she was licking away at another one. Startled, Peter looked back at the candy stand that he'd passed a short while ago and then into Veronica's face. She smiled innocently at him but tugged at his jacket as she moved them both along into safer territory.

Well, well, he was never sure what to do when Veronica went foraging, but the candy lay enticingly in his hand with its sour-sweet apricot smell, so he licked at it guiltily at first, then took a joyful chew, and hurried along a little faster.

At the corner, they turned and began skating in earnest under the shade of the elevated train up above. There was a trolley ahead of them, and Veronica motioned with her head as her skates began gathering speed. The trolley stopped, people got off and on, and breathlessly, they reached it just as it began moving again. Veronica held on to the back

of the trolley with one hand and continued holding
her candy with the other. But Peter let his drop, as
he held on with both hands. This was only the second time he'd hooked onto the outside of a trolley,
and all the warnings and dire prophecies of grownups through all his twelve years about what happened to children who snuck rides on the backs of
trolleys still clamored at him from inside his brain.

The trolley jerked to a start and yanked them
along over the cobblestone streets, faster, faster,
faster. It was horrible, terrifying, glorious. Veronica
sang, "Over hill, over dale, as we hit the dusty trail."
His eyes were glued to the back of the trolley. He
was afraid to look at her, but her voice was reassur-
ing, and he laughed a short, hysterical laugh and
then concentrated on holding on as hard as he could.

They had been friends for only a few months. Before that, they were enemies. That was back in P. S.
63 when they were both in eighth grade. He had
just moved into the neighborhood and found Veronica in his class. The biggest bully in the world, the
other kids told him, bigger, stronger, fiercer than
anybody else. She'd beat anybody up for nothing,
they said, and nobody yet had been able to stop
her. Well, he'd stopped her all right. He'd teased
her and made up funny jingles about her, and she'd
chased him for weeks until he got a couple of other
boys to help beat her up. And that's how the friendship began. Because after it was all over, he knew
he had done a terrible thing, the worst thing he'd

ever done in his whole life. He'd ganged up on one person, and that person a girl too. So he'd apologized and offered to let her smack him. And she stood there with her fists clenched, towering over him. And at first she looked like she was going to hit him, and then she looked like she was going to cry, and then she started laughing, and all of a sudden, they were friends.

The trolley jerked to a stop, and Peter and Veronica let go, moving back a few feet, just in case the driver decided to come out and have a look. More passengers got on and off, the bell clanged, and they were off again. Above them, the elevated trains screeched along, and beneath them, the ground flew out from under their skates.

After a while, the trolley stopped suddenly in the middle of the street and Veronica yelled, "Let's go!" They began racing off as they heard the driver's footsteps and his shouts behind them. Down a side street, around a corner, along another street they sped. Breathlessly, Peter raced after Veronica, the wind hitting his face so hard that he had to gasp for breath, swallowing painful, icy patches of air.

There was a pain in his throat that brought whirling lights to his eyes, and he headed into a lamppost, catching it with both arms and curling around it and around it and around it, until it held him finally, gasping but at rest.

She came back and circled him. "Gee, that was great!" she said.

Peter moved over, and she came and leaned with him against the post. They looked at each other and began laughing. She pushed him. He tottered but did not fall. He butted her and down she went, still laughing.

They sat for a few moments on the curb, their feet motionless and heavy.

Peter looked around him and said tentatively, "Say, I know where we are."

"Where?"

"My Uncle Jake's store is around here someplace. Come on!"

He got up and began skating, and Veronica followed. It was cold and beginning to darken. The lights went on, and Peter shivered and knew it was time to go home.

"I gotta go home," Veronica shouted, and Peter cried, "O.K., but let's just find my uncle's store."

They found it, a few blocks down. It was a little store, and outside on the glass pane it said, JAKE'S KNISHES.

"Come on, let's go in," Peter said. He opened the door, and the warm fragrance of steam heat and knishes felt like the promised land.

"I'll wait for you outside," Veronica said.

"Oh, come on," Peter said, grabbing her hand and pulling her along with him.

A small man at the counter looked up and smiled. "Peter," he cried. "Hello, Peter."

"Hello, Uncle Jake," Peter said. He let go of Veronica's hand and skated up to the counter.

"I'm just closing up," said Uncle Jake. "What are you doing here?"

"My friend and I were skating."

"Good!" said Uncle Jake. "Hello," he said, smiling at Veronica, who leaned against the door. "And how's Mama?" he continued to Peter.

"Oh, she's fine."

"And Papa?"

"He's fine."

"And Rosalie?"

"Fine."

"Anything new with Rosalie?"

"What do you mean new?"

"I mean how's her boy friend?"

"Oh, he's fine."

"Anything new with her boy friend?"

"What do you mean new?"

"Nothing new." Uncle Jake sighed. "So come in, come in," he shouted heartily to Veronica, who was still leaning against the door. "Very nice of you to come see me, both of you. Do you want a knish?"

"Boy, do I!" said Peter.

"What kind?"

"Do you have any kasha left?"

Uncle Jake inspected the tray under the counter, selected one, wrapped it in a napkin, and handed it to Peter.

"And you, girlie, what would you like? We've got kasha, cabbage, and potato left."

"What's a knish?" Veronica asked.

"What's a knish?" Uncle Jake repeated. "You mean you never ate a knish?"

Veronica shook her head.

"Potato," said Uncle Jake, wrapping one up in a napkin. "Here, take a potato." He reached over the counter, and Veronica took it from him and looked at it, but did not eat it.

"Go ahead, eat," Uncle Jake urged.

Veronica took a little nibble. Uncle Jake and Peter watched her as she slowly chewed and then swallowed. She took another bite. "Hey, it's good," she said.

Peter finished his and licked some pieces of the salty pastry left in his napkin. Uncle Jake silently handed him another one.

"What's in yours?" asked Veronica.

"Kasha."

"What's that?"

Peter held his out and she took a bite, made a face, and said, "I like mine better."

"That's because you're just beginning," said Uncle Jake, holding out another potato knish toward her. "After a while, you'll like the kasha too."

"Well, I guess we'd better be going now," said Peter.

"That's right. It's getting dark, and Mama'll be

looking for you. Say hello from me. I'll come by maybe Sunday.

"Goody-by, Uncle Jake, and thanks for the knishes."

"Good-by," Veronica murmured, "and thank-you."

"Good-by. Nice meeting you, and come again," said Uncle Jake.

Outside, the cold, March night flew at them and they held the remains of their hot knishes under their noses, enjoying the mingling of the two worlds of warm and cold.

"He's nice, your uncle," Veronica said, sighing, "nicer than my uncle."

"I've got a lot of uncles," said Peter, "but Uncle Jake's the nicest. What's your uncle?"

"Uncle Charles. He's got a diner near West Farms."

Peter stopped smelling the fading warmth of his knish. "Let's go visit him sometime."

"Well," Veronica said carefully, "my mother's not talking to him. I haven't seen him for a couple of years, but once he gave us a big lemon meringue pie." She began skating, and Peter swallowed the remains of his knish and hurried along beside her.

"Well, here goes," he said.

A raindrop fell on his nose, then another, and then another.

"It's raining," Veronica chortled, and by the time they had hooked onto a trolley for the return trip, the rain had plastered their hair down on their heads, run down the collars of their jackets, and transformed the streets into a glistening pool of lights.

"You are my sunshine, my only sunshine," Veronica sang, and Peter laughed and held on with both hands.

2

"Peter?"

He laid the skates down in the hall, shook off the top layer of raindrops from every part of him, pulled his wet handkerchief out of his wet pocket, dabbed at his face, and quickly smoothed his hair. It was all futile anyway, he knew, because she was sure to fuss.

He walked into the living room and braced himself. A strange woman sat on the couch and she smiled and nodded at him. But Mama got up from her chair and said, "What happened to you? You're soaking wet. Where were you?"

"Oh . . . around," Peter said vaguely, and then added hopefully, "I better go change."

"Take off your shoes and socks right away," Mama said sharply. If the lady wasn't there, she would have gone on for a while, but out of politeness for her guest she held off mentioning all the other articles of clothing, seen and unseen, that should be removed.

"This is my boy," she said to the guest, "my Peter. You remember Mrs. Rappaport, don't you, Peter?"

"Uh, I think so," Peter said politely. "How do you do, Mrs. Rappaport."

"Nice boy," Mrs. Rappaport said, smiling to Mama. "How old is he?"

"Twelve." Mama rested a warm, plump hand on his shoulder. "He'll be thirteen in May."

"Like my grandson," Mrs. Rappaport said, "Rachel's boy. But he's much taller."

Mama's hand stiffened on his shoulder, and he said, "I better go change, Mama."

"You should give him lots of milk," Mrs. Rappaport said, "and liver. He'd grow taller if he ate liver."

"*Kinnahura*, he eats fine," Mama said coldly, "and he's growing fast. He's like my brother, Irving. He didn't grow until he was thirteen and now he's over six feet. It'll be the same with my Peter."

Peter squirmed unhappily under Mama's hand. He didn't like being short, and every time Mama said how fast he was growing—and she'd been saying it for years—he felt worse.

"I better go change," he said.

But Mama's hand held him. "Reads all the time," Mama said. "Such books! You wouldn't believe it."

"My grandson too," Mrs. Rappaport said airily.

"The smartest one in the class," Mama continued.

Peter writhed desperately, and said, "Ma, I better . . ."

"Like my grandson," echoed Mrs. Rappaport.

"Been on the honor roll every single term since he started school," Mama said.

There was no response from Mrs. Rappaport.

"I saved them," Mama said, pressing her advantage. "I'll show them to you."

"Very nice," Mrs. Rappaport said coldly. She looked at Peter. "You go to *cheder?*" she asked.

"Uh, huh."

"And you should hear what the Hebrew School teacher said to me last week," said Mama. "He said my Peter's the best, that's just what he said, the best student he ever had. He said Peter could get a scholarship to the Yeshiva if he wanted, and study to be a rabbi."

Mrs. Rappaport stood up. "I'm going," she said

"No, no," Mama said. "Stay a while. Sol should be home from synagogue soon."

Mrs. Rappaport remained standing, but she said to Peter, "It's raining outside?"

"Pouring," Peter said.

"How come you went out on such a day?"

"Library?" Mama murmured.

"No, I was skating with my friend," Peter said, "and it wasn't raining when we started."

"Skating?" Mrs. Rappaport said, raising her eyebrows. She sat down. "Skating? A big boy like you."

Mama's hand stiffened again on his shoulder.

"Lots of kids my age do," Peter said uncomfortably. "My friend is thirteen and a half."

"A Jewish boy?" asked Mrs. Rappaport.

"No, a girl."

"A Jewish girl?"

"No . . ."

"Peter," Mama cried, "go change! You're soaking wet. Why are you standing there like that?" She gave him a little push toward his bedroom, and as he hurried off he heard Mrs. Rappaport say, "A very nice boy, but you got to be careful. Even at his age, you never know . . ."

Everything was wet. Peter pulled all his clothes off and put on dry things. But he stayed in his room and wandered around restlessly. After a while he opened the door a crack and listened. He could hear voices from the living room, Papa's voice too, but she was still there so he closed the door again. Wouldn't she ever go home?

He moved over to the bookcase and pulled out one of his library books, a big one entitled *Snakes and Other Reptiles,* and settled down at his desk. But he didn't feel like reading now, so he put it back and noticed a couple of stamps on the floor. Mama had been cleaning again, yanking out his stamp album and all his other books in her endless pursuit of fugitive specks of dust. He clenched his teeth, and then suddenly his heart began pounding as he wondered if she'd found it. Quickly he pulled out the *M* volume of the *Wonderland of Knowledge* encyclopedia, opened to page 117, and relaxed. His pamphlet, sent to him through the mail for twenty-five cents, and entitled "Basic Body Building Exercises for Boys," lay there untouched. But he'd better find another place for it. Where though? Was there any place safe from Mama? His chest of drawers? No. She was continually arranging and rearranging his socks and underwear. The closet? No. She liked to take all the clothes out and vacuum every couple of months. Under his mattress? Even that was no good, because she had this thing about bedbugs and was forever spraying Flit on the mattress and the bedsprings.

Peter sat down on the bed and allowed himself a short but intense moment of self-pity. Was there no place in the whole world that belonged to him and only him? What about the desk? He had inherited the desk from cousin Jeffrey who was now grown-up and married. It had a lock in the middle drawer but no key. But he could have a key made for it, couldn't he? Maybe Marv could help him remove the lock from the desk. Then he could take it over to the locksmith and have a key made. Beautiful!

Peter grinned, but his smile faded as another problem presented itself. Where would he keep the key? Well—maybe wear it around his neck. No. He hated things around his neck. Maybe over at Marv's house, and he could go and get it whenever he needed it. But Marv had a mother, too, who was

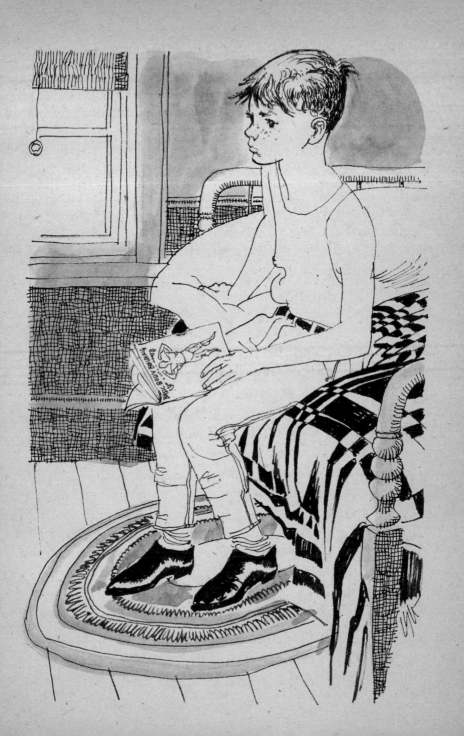

always cleaning. There was Jack Tarr whose mother was dead, but he lived over on 166th Street and that was too far away.

So—where could he keep the key: in his shoe, maybe, or . . . wonderful . . . now he had it. Quickly he opened his window and reached out, feeling around the side of the building until he found the old hook. A wash line had once hung there, but now only the hook remained. He could hang the key on a string and suspend it from the hook. She'd never find it there.

In the meantime, Peter put the pamphlet back in the *M* volume and replaced it on the shelf. Since she'd just dusted, he figured he had about a week's grace, and in that time he'd make sure to get a key.

He picked the stamps up off the floor, took out his stamp album, and settled himself at the desk. One of the stamps was from French Equatorial Africa and the other from Liechtenstein. He put a fresh stamp hinge on each of them and pasted them back in their places. He'd been saving stamps since he was nine, and at first Mama had said it was a waste of time and money. But he kept reminding her in the beginning that President Roosevelt also saved stamps and that helped. Last year, when he won second prize in a stamp tournament, she became enthusiastic. That was one thing about Mama. Prizes always made her enthusiastic.

He turned to his United States stamps and studied his commemorative collection, noting lovingly his

first-day cover of the World's Fair stamp issued in
1939, two years ago. He'd gotten it from Joey Pincus
and it had cost him twelve stamps from Brazil,
three from Canada, four from the Union of South
Africa, and fifty cents besides.

Somebody knocked on his door. Peter braced himself and said suspiciously, "Who is it?"

"Me, cookie," Rosalie said. "Can I come in?"

"Oh, Rosalie!" Peter jumped up and opened the
door for her. "Come on in. Is she still there?" he
whispered.

His sister's usually cheerful face looked grim. "Yes,"
she said, closing the door behind her, "the *yenta!*"

Peter studied his sister's face sympathetically. Mrs.
Rappaport probably had been asking her questions
about Bernard, her boy friend. She'd been going out
with Bernard for nearly a year now, but nothing
much seemed to be happening.

Rosalie was twenty-three and worked as a book-
keeper for a button business. She was small, a little
on the plump side, and her broad, pink-cheeked
face had a thoughtful, patient look. People said she
was a "sweet girl," which meant that they didn't
think she was pretty.

"Anyway," Rosalie said, "what's my favorite
brother up to?"

"Oh, just looking at my stamps," Peter said, motioning to the album.

Rosalie moved over to the desk and stood, studying the stamps. "Mmm," she said approvingly, "any new ones?"

"No, I've been so busy lately, I haven't had a chance."

"You're really working hard these days, aren't you, honey, getting ready for the bar mitzvah?" Rosalie patted his shoulder, and her eyes were tender. "My little brother, growing up so fast."

Peter moved away carefully. Rosalie was great and all that, but like Mama, she got mushy at times.

"Is Bernard coming tonight?" he asked, changing the subject. Bernard had been coming every Friday night for dinner for quite some time, so it was a safe question.

"Yes," Rosalie said, looking at her watch. "He'll be here in a few minutes, so I'd better get ready. We're supposed to go to a concert tonight, but if that woman doesn't leave, we'll never have time to eat."

They both heard the sound of a door bang, and smiled at each other in relief. Peter opened the door to his room and shouted, "Is she gone, Mama?" He walked into the living room. Mrs. Rappaport was just standing up, putting on her coat.

"No, she's not gone," said Mrs. Rappaport acidly, "but she's going now."

"Shame on you, Peter," Mama said weakly. Then she took Mrs. Rappaport's hand, and said, "You know how it is. He's hungry and—"

"Yes," said Mrs. Rappaport loftily, "I know how

it is. Good-by, Peter. Be a good boy and don't disgrace your parents. Good-by. Good-by."

Mama walked her to the door, and when she came back her face was furious. "Such terrible manners!" she yelled. "I was so ashamed, I could have fallen through the floor."

"Well, I heard the door slam so I thought she'd left," Peter said defensively. "Besides, I didn't like her."

"So what difference does that make?" Mama answered. "I don't like her either, always bragging about her grandson, the big *schlemiel,* but still, she's a guest in the house, and that's no way to treat guests. Now she'll tell everybody what a bad boy I've got."

"Who cares what she says?"

"I care."

The door opened and Peter's father came into the room. "She's gone? Thank goodness. I had to run out for a breath of air. Ah—Peter! How's my boy?"

"Fine, Papa."

"He's not fine," said Mama. "He was fresh to Mrs. Rappaport and he runs around all the time with a girl—a terrible girl—and you've got to tell him to stop."

"Stop!" said Papa.

He and Peter began laughing. Mama raised a finger in the air and prepared to explode, but then the doorbell rang and Mama's hand dropped, and her face assumed that special eager look it had whenever a boy friend arrived for Rosalie.

"I'll talk to you later," she hissed, and then in a louder voice, a sweeter voice, she called, "Rosalie . . . go, Rosalie, open the door. It's Bernard."

Saved by the bell, Peter thought, as he returned to his room to put away his stamp album and to make certain that the *M* volume of the *Wonderland of Knowledge* wasn't sticking out any further than its companions.

3

Marv Green was a genius. Peter knew this with absolute certainty. He knew with equal certainty that nobody else, including Marv and his family, believed this to be the case.

Sunday at nine, a drizzling, blowy Sunday, Peter crossed the street and headed for Marv's house. There were only two one-family houses on the street, and Marv lived in one of them. All the other houses were apartment houses, and the two small gray brick buildings huddled together between their giant neighbors, attached like ancient, wizened Siamese twins.

Both houses had wooden staircases leading up to the front entrances. One of the houses had a small plot of land on the side of the staircase with a neat border of privet hedges framing it. The other house had a moat with a bridge over it constructed of cement with stones, pieces of flowerpots, broken crockery, and soda bottle tops embedded in it. The moat was empty now except for puddles, but in the summer it would be converted into the only swimming pool in the entire neighborhood.

Peter hurried across the bridge and down the small set of stairs leading to the basement. The door was open, as usual, and Peter passed quickly through the dark basement and out through the back into the yard. Here Marv could generally be found. Sometimes Peter wondered what would have happened to Marv if his family had lived in an apartment house and there had been no yard for him to operate out of. But it was an impossible thought—like trying to think of an eagle without the sky or a whale without water.

Marv was a builder. He built all the time. Even when he wasn't building, he was thinking about building. In school, he was in the dumb class because his teachers said he just wouldn't pay attention. He failed in math, but had no difficulty in constructing the complicated mechanical elevator that stood twelve feet high over in one corner of the yard. The elevator had taken Marv only three months to build. Peter, who was always the star pupil in his math classes, had offered to help, but had found all the calculations too difficult for him to fathom. Marv had his own system of figuring that left Peter far behind. But Marv was always patient and tolerant, so Peter carried the wood, hammered the nails, and put the screws and pulleys where he was told.

Now that the elevator was finished, Marv planned on putting a building around it. He was there in the yard, as Peter had expected, but his eighteen-year-old sister, Frances, was there too. Marv had another sister, Betsy, who was fifteen, and so pretty that Peter felt uncomfortable every time she spoke to him. Frances was pretty too, he supposed, but most of the time he saw her, she was generally shouting at Marv, and this morning was no exception.

"I told you this part of the yard was mine," she was yelling, "and if I told you once, I told you a hundred times."

"I know, I know," Marv was saying sadly. "I'm sorry. I forgot, but next time."

"Next time!" Frances hissed between her teeth. "It's always next time. First you dug up all my daffodils when you made that crazy goldfish pool. Then you built that stupid dog palace for Queenie, and she never even goes into it, and you spoiled the iris. Then you built that horrible moat outside, and all the cats keep drowning in it. . . ."

"Only two," Marv corrected gently.

". . . and pulled up all the rosebushes. Then those sappy revolving doors going nowhere over *my* cannas, and now that elevator. What do you need an elevator for? There's nothing above it. Just look at this yard. It's disgusting. I'm ashamed to bring anyone home for fear they'll look out the window and think this is a lunatic asylum. And every time I plant something, you spoil it."

"Frances," Marv said patiently, "would you like me to make you a window box?"

"*No!*" screamed Frances.

"Frances," Marv continued, blinking at the force of his sister's cry, "I'll make you two window boxes. You can have them outside your bedroom windows and they'll be safe there."

"I don't want window boxes," Frances shouted. "I just want a little piece of this yard. That's all I want."

"Frances," Marv continued dreamily, "I can make you two window boxes, and in one I can carve FRANCES and in the other I can carve GREEN. I can inlay pieces of blue glass in the FRANCES, and maybe pink glass in the GREEN, or maybe green glass (Marv chuckled), and I can have a light inside that goes on and off . . ."

"Ma!" Frances yelled desperately, "Ma!"

A window over the yard opened, and Mrs. Green stuck her head out. "Shh, Frances," she said. "You'll wake Papa. Hello, Peter."

"Mama," Frances cried, "will you please make him stop ruining my flowers?"

"Shh," said Mrs. Green, "come inside, children. It's raining outside. You'll get wet."

"Mama," Frances continued stubbornly, "I've got as much right to this yard as he has. And if you don't figure out a way to make him respect my rights, I'll have to take some kind of drastic action." She pointed a finger dramatically at Marv and stood like an accusing angel, waiting for her mother to speak.

Mrs. Green hesitated, looked around her uncomfortably, and then brightened. "Let's have breakfast," she said happily. "I'll make pancakes."

"Oh, Ma!" Frances yelled. She stamped her foot and ran out of the yard, banging the cellar door behind her.

Mrs. Green sighed. "She's very high-strung," she said in explanation to Peter. "Come inside, Marvin, and have breakfast."

"Oh, Ma, I don't have the time," Marv said. "Just throw me down a roll and butter, cheese and onion, and I'll eat it down here."

Mrs. Green nodded, smiled, and withdrew, closing the window behind her. It wasn't so much, Peter knew, that Marv's mother appreciated his accomplishments. Any time Marv would show her his current creation, she'd say something like, "Fine, but don't fall" or "Very good, but put on a sweater. You'll catch cold." It was just that she was a gentle, easygoing woman who avoided arguments more than anything else. As long as Marv was happy and didn't make too much noise, she was satisfied.

In a little while, Marv, munching away on his roll, began laying out the foundation for the new building. There was no problem finding wood. For years, long before Peter had known him, Marv had been building, and the yard looked like an archaeologist's dream, with layers and sublayers of the ruins of former glories. Wood from the top layers of these ancient relics would be gathered by Marv for new projects.

By the end of the morning, they had laid the floor and were working on the upright posts for the walls. The rain had stopped, and the air smelled clean and full of the sweetness of wet wood.

Mr. Green came through the cellar door, and Marv yelled, "Pa, look, Pa! We've got the floor laid."

Mr. Green walked over to the construction site, inspected the floor, and chuckled. He was a very busy man, Marv's father, a baker, who spent long hours after work involved in his union. Lately he hadn't been feeling well and his face was pale and thin.

"Very good," he said, "and maybe sometime today, when you get a chance, you can look at the hot-water faucet in the bathroom sink. It's leaking again."

Marv hit his head. "I keep forgetting to buy a washer," he said. "Tomorrow I'll pick one up after school."

"Fine!" Mr. Green said, and laid a hand on Marv's shoulder. "But also, how about trying to let Frances have a piece of the yard too? She's upset and I can't blame her. You know, Marv, she likes flowers and she should have a chance to use the yard too."

Marv hung his head. A word from his father was like ten thousand words from his mother.

"So how about it?" Mr. Green said gently. "You'll try, Marvin?"

"I'll try, Papa," Marv said earnestly, "I'll really try.

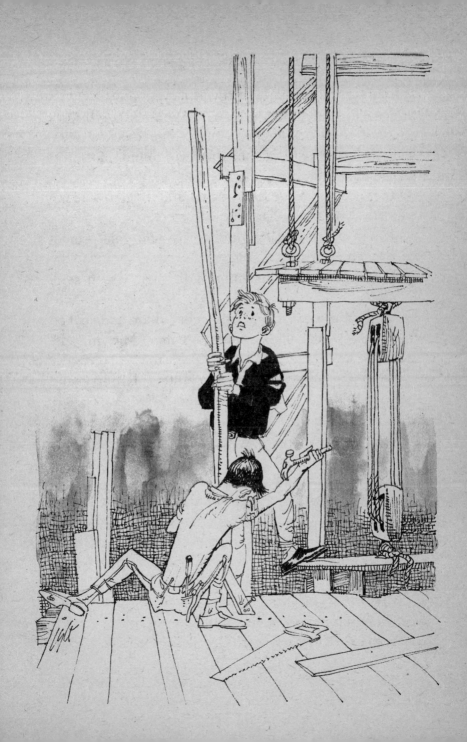

Maybe I should build a little fence around her part of the yard and then I won't forget." Marv brightened. "I've got some posts and some chicken wire, and I'll make one—no—maybe two round plots just for her."

"Good boy," Mr. Green said, and began walking back toward the cellar.

"Papa," Marv said longingly, "are you going somewhere, Papa?"

"I have to go to the union hall," Mr. Green said.

"Oh."

Mr. Green hesitated at the cellar door and looked back at his son. "You want to come, Marvin?" he asked.

"Sure, Pa. It'll take me a minute. I'll hurry and clean up." Marv's voice was eager.

Mr. Green smiled. "Good. I won't have too much to do there, and maybe afterward we'll go somewhere."

"There's a new boat down at the navy yard," Marv said hungrily. "I saw it in the paper. It's an aircraft carrier, and they let you go on it."

"So we'll go see the new boat," said Mr. Green. He walked through the door, and Marv quickly began assembling his tools.

"Guess I'll go home," Peter said brightly, wondering if he might be invited along.

"You can stay and work if you like," Marv said.

"Well, I'm not going to stay by myself," Peter said, and waited.

Marv avoided his eyes. "How about tomorrow, then?"

"Tomorrow I have to go to *cheder*, but today I don't have anything to do."

Marv picked up his tools and began hurrying across the yard. It was plain that Peter was not going to be invited along.

"I'm going home," he repeated, and followed Marv out of the yard.

In the cellar, Marv laid his tools down and said meekly, "I'm sorry, Peter, but . . . well . . ."

"Oh, forget it," Peter said, hiding his disappointment. He knew Marv had very little time alone with his father. "I'll see you around."

He walked through the cellar out to the front, across the little bridge, and back to his own house. Slowly he climbed the stairs of the stoop and wondered what to do next. Maybe he'd just mention the boat to his own father.

Both of his parents were in the kitchen. His mother was busy cooking, and his father sat with a big book in front of him at the kitchen table.

"Papa," Peter said, "there's a new boat at the navy yard. Do you want to go see it?"

His father looked up at him. "A boat?" he asked. "Why do you want to look at a boat?"

"Don't bother your father," his mother said. "Let him rest."

"It's a big one, an aircraft carrier," Peter said

lamely. "Marv and his father are going so I thought . . ."

Papa smiled but shook his head. "No, I don't think I'd like to go. But you go ahead with them." He began reading again,

Peter thought for a moment and then went off to find his skates.

"Where are you going, Peter?" his mother called as he passed the kitchen on his way out.

"Skating."

"I told her already you couldn't go."

"Told who?"

"That girl."

Peter came into the kitchen. "Was Veronica here this morning? Why didn't you tell me?"

His mother ran water in the sink. "You didn't ask."

"Ma," Peter cried, "why didn't you tell her where I was?"

"I didn't know where you were."

"But I told you I was going to Marv's house."

"I forgot."

"Mama," Peter said angrily, "what have you got against her? What did she ever do to you?"

He dropped his skates on the floor, and his father looked up, startled, from his book.

"Now you're disturbing your father. Why don't you go and play with Marvin?"

"Now you want me to play with Marvin, but you used to say I shouldn't play with Marvin because he was stupid. How come you changed your mind all

of a sudden? How come now you want me to play
with Marvin?"

"Because," said his mother, turning off the water
and facing him angrily, "Marvin may not be the
smartest boy in the world, but he's still a nice boy—
a big difference between Marvin and that crazy,
wild, fresh girl you've been hanging around with all
of a sudden. And let me ask you a question: what
do you have in common with such a girl, a boy like
you, a smart, well-brought-up, Jewish boy with a
. . . a . . ."

"That's it, isn't it?" Peter yelled triumphantly. "It's
because she's not Jewish, isn't it? Mama, you're prejudiced, that's what you are."

Peter's father closed his book and sighed.

"Prejudiced! I'm prejudiced!" shouted Mrs. Wedemeyer. "That I should live to see the day that my
own son stands there to my face and calls me prejudiced! And for what? For an ignorant, stupid, ugly
stranger."

"She's not stupid and she's not ignorant and she's
my friend. You wouldn't care if she was the most
beautiful genius in the whole world. It's just that
she's not Jewish. Well, she's my friend and I like
her and I don't care what she is."

His father began chuckling. "Thine own friend,
forsake not," he quoted in Yiddish. Peter's father
always seemed to have a proverb handy, culled from
all the years poring over his religious books. "You're
making a fuss over nothing, Jennie. Leave the boy

alone. He's old enough now to pick his own friends. Don't ask for trouble."

There was a moment of silence. Mr. Wedemeyer opened his book again, and Peter picked up his skates. Then his mother exploded.

"Some father you are!" she shouted at her husband. "You sit there all the time with your nose in a book and you don't take any interest in him. Why don't you go places with him, like right now. Take him out to see . . . to see that boat."

"I don't care for boats," Mr. Wedemeyer said pleasantly.

"You don't care where he goes or who he plays with. You don't know the kind of girl this is. She's a juvenile delinquent, that's what she is. I found out. I asked around in the neighborhood. He thinks I don't know what she is, but I look out for him. But you, all you're interested in is sitting there reading the same books over and over again.

Mr. Wedemeyer rose, picked up his book, and, speaking in Yiddish, said with dignity:

"It is better to dwell in a corner of the housetop
 Than in a house in common with a contentious woman."

As he left the room, Mrs. Wedemeyer burst into tears, and Peter grabbed his skates and ran.

4

"I changed my mind," Veronica said. "I'm not going in."

Peter had his hand on the door, but he turned around and said irritably, "Why not?" What a day this was turning out to be! First that scene with his mother, then Stanley blubbering away, and now, after skating miles and miles down to West Farms, Veronica was going to give him a hard time.

"Why not?" he demanded again.

She shrugged her shoulders. "Wasn't my idea in the first place. You talked me into it, and I just don't want to go in. That's all! Now let's go."

The door of the diner opened, and Peter had to step to one side as a big man with a toothpick in his mouth came through the door. Before the door closed again, Peter caught a glimpse of the inside of the diner and got a warm, fragrant sniff of hamburgers and onions. Maybe Veronica had eaten lunch, but he hadn't, and it reinforced his desire to act as peacemaker between Veronica and her kin.

The man proceeded slowly down the stairs, and Peter said persuasively, "Let's just take a look inside. We don't have to stay."

"No!"

"What have you got to lose? Your uncle will probably be so happy to see you that he'll . . ." Peter licked his lips in anticipation of the way in which Veronica's uncle would show his joy at the sudden appearance of his niece.

"No!"

"Why not?"

"Because I haven't seen him for four years, and the last time he came he fought with my mother, so why should I go out of my way to see him?"

Veronica's parents were divorced. Her mother had remarried, and her father lived in Las Vegas with his second wife. Veronica hadn't seen her father since she was little. She and her sister, Mary Rose, were children of her mother's first marriage, while Stanley was her half brother. The uncle, whose diner they were standing in front of, was her father's older brother.

"Well, let's just go in, and see what he has to say."

"No!"

"You shouldn't be so hardhearted, Veronica. Let bygones be bygones," Peter said righteously. "I bet he's sorry. After all, we all make mistakes, and if he's sorry, you shouldn't go on like that, carrying grudges. Give him a break."

Veronica snorted, but she looked hesitantly at the door.

"Come on, we'll try him out," Peter said, taking her hand and pulling her up the stairs. "Let's see what he has to say for himself."

"If he says one thing about my mother . . ." Veronica said fiercely, but she allowed Peter to haul her up the stairs with him, through the door and into the diner.

They stood for a moment inside the door, expanding in the warmth and looking around them. There were some booths against the wall and a long counter with a row of seats that ran down the length of the room. Peter, holding Veronica's hand, skated her over to two unoccupied seats at the counter. There was a tall, blond, teen-aged boy behind the counter, and Veronica nudged Peter, and whispered, "That's Charles, Jr."

"Who's Charles, Jr.?" Peter asked, enjoying the view of three or four pies with triangular pieces cut out of them.

"The youngest one. My uncle has two boys—August and Charles, Jr."

"Oh." Peter inspected the case that held a large chocolate cake, an equally large coconut layer cake, and a variety of doughnuts. After a while, Charles, Jr., came over to them and said, "Yes?"

Peter finished his appraisal of the baked apples,

smiled at Charles, Jr., turned a little toward Veronica, and waited.

But Charles, Jr., just looked at the two of them blankly and said, "What do you want?"

"Let's go," said Veronica, beginning to rise.

"Just a minute," Peter said, holding her down and catching a fleeting glimpse of some apple turnovers off in the distance. "Is Mr. Ganz around?"

"My father? Yes, he's in the back."

"Could we see him, please?" Peter said, trying to sound important.

Charles, Jr., poked his head around the partition that separated the kitchen from the front and said, "Pa, there's a kid here who wants to see you."

"What did you do that for?" Veronica hissed.

Peter let his eyes move from the tray of Jell-O to the one filled with rice pudding and murmured gently, "Just give him a chance."

A very tall, powerful, blond man emerged from the kitchen. His son motioned in their direction, and Veronica's uncle approached them.

"You wanted to see me?" he said.

Peter smiled benignly at him, and then motioned with his head at Veronica, and waited for the reconciliation scene.

Mr. Ganz looked at Veronica then back at Peter. "Well, what is it?" he asked impatiently.

Peter was astonished. Veronica's uncle did not know who she was. Why, in his family, everybody knew everybody else down to the third cousins, four times removed. He could feel Veronica stiffen next to him, and he said quickly, "Uh, could I have a glass of water, please?"

Mr. Ganz impatiently filled a glass with water and slapped it down on the counter. "Now what's up?" he demanded.

Peter sipped his water, glanced at Veronica with her eyes down on the counter, and beyond her to a case filled with Danish pastries.

"Nice place you got here—Mr. Ganz?"

"How do you know my name?" said the man suspiciously.

"That your boy over there?" Peter asked.

Mr. Ganz's eyes narrowed.

"Nice boy," Peter said nervously. "Have you got any girls?"

"Look, who sent you over here?" Veronica's uncle said, bending over him.

"Nobody. I just wondered if you had any daughters or maybe nieces, because it's nice having girls in a family," Peter said lamely.

"I'm going," Veronica said, rising.

Veronica's uncle put out a huge hand and caught Peter's jacket with it.

"What do you want, kid? What kind of a game are you playing?"

"Let him go!" Veronica yelled. She pushed her uncle's hand away, and Peter said sadly, "O.K., Veronica, you're right. Let's go."

"Veronica?" said Mr. Ganz. He came quickly

around the counter and loomed above them just as they reached the door. "Veronica?" he said to Veronica. "Are you Veronica?"

"Yes," said Veronica, trying to skate around him to the door.

"Veronica Ganz?" He put his hand on her shoulder and looked at her. She struggled for a moment and then stood there with her eyes on the ground.

"Well, what do you know," said Mr. Ganz slowly. "It's Veronica."

He propelled her over to one of the tables and eased her into a seat. Then he sat down across from her and suddenly began grinning. "The image of Frank," he said. "The image of him."

"You didn't know who I was," Veronica said, stubbornly keeping her eyes away from his.

"Just for the minute," said her uncle, "and that kid kept on talking. I didn't know what he was up to."

He looked up at Peter who had slowly followed them over to the table. "Come here, boy, sit down." Peter sat down carefully next to Veronica, and Mr. Ganz laughed and said, "Well, that's a good joke on me. Do I have any girls in my family?" He laughed a loud, hearty laugh and leaned over to poke Peter's shoulder. "You're a real comedian, son. What's your name?"

"Peter Wedemeyer, sir."

"Yes, sir, Peter Wedemeyer, you're a real comedian." Veronica's uncle laughed some more. Then he

looked Veronica over again and said, "Wait till I write your father and tell how his beautiful daughter came to visit me and played a joke on me."

Veronica's face turned red, but she still kept her eyes down and didn't say anything.

"You know, just the other day I was saying to your Aunt Margaret that you and Mary Jane must be grown-up now, and that one of these days I was just going to have to come over and see the two of you. Just the other day I said it. Isn't that funny?"

"Her name is Mary Rose, not Mary Jane," Veronica said between her teeth.

"That's what I said—Mary Rose, and here you are. Isn't that great! So many times I wanted to run over and see the two of you, I can't tell you."

"But you never did," Veronica said, looking up at him finally, with a serious face.

"Aw, honey, don't be like that," Uncle Charles said, leaning toward her. "Lots of things a kid like you doesn't understand. But now here we are together, so how about giving your uncle a big, sweet smile."

Veronica just looked at him without smiling.

"She's shy," Peter murmured.

"Shy, is she, my beautiful niece?" Uncle Charles reached over and patted Veronica's cheek. "I bet she doesn't have any teeth—that's why she's not smiling."

Veronica struggled for a moment, but then her face grew very red and she burst out laughing. Peter did, too, and so did Uncle Charles.

"That's better," Uncle Charles said comfortably,

rumpling her hair. "And how about some lunch, something superduper for my superduper niece?"

"I had lunch," said Veronica.

"I didn't," Peter said happily.

Peter had two hamburgers, a piece of apple pie, and a Coke. Veronica refused to eat anything. But after Peter had finished eating, and the two of them stood up, ready to go, Uncle Charles said, "Just a minute." He went into the kitchen and returned with a big, flat, white box.

"Some things maybe I don't remember so well," he said, "but some things I do. Is lemon meringue pie still your favorite?" he asked Veronica.

Veronica's eyes shone.

"Here," he said, holding the box out toward her, "for you and Mary Rose."

Veronica's hands remained at her side. "And Stanley too?" she asked tensely.

"And Stanley too," Uncle Charles said gently. She took the box then, and Uncle Charles put an arm around her shoulder and said, "You're a good girl, Veronica. You were very good to come and see me, and after this, I won't wait for you to come. I'll be by to see you and Mary Rose real soon. So give her a kiss from me, and . . . and . . . say hello to your mother."

Veronica was halfway up the block before Peter caught up with her.

"He's a pretty nice guy, your uncle," Peter said, "and watch out, you'll drop the box."

Veronica was holding it with two fingers crooked under the string. Her face was glowing, and she giggled and said, "I thought he was going to break your neck when you said that about him having any girls in his family. What a nut you are!"

"Uh, huh," said Peter, his mind on more important matters. "But how are we going to get home with that. We'll never make it skating. We better take the trolley. Do you have any money?"

"No—you?"

"I've only got a nickel, so why don't you go back and get a nickel from your uncle."

"No," Veronica said very firmly. "We'll skate."

"We'd never make it."

She looked at him appraisingly. "Maybe," she said thoughtfully, "if we both get on the streetcar together, and you stoop down a little and hold my hand, the driver might think you were my kid brother."

"I don't look like a five-year-old," Peter said, suddenly close to tears.

"No, no, I don't mean that," Veronica said quickly. "Only I'm so tall. That's what I mean. It's me—I'm so big that maybe—aw gee, Peter—I didn't mean anything. My mother didn't start paying for Mary Rose on the streetcar until she was ten, and she was always tall for her age. Look, let's just forget it and skate home. Or, how about this . . ."

"The trolley's coming," Peter said, motioning down the track. "Hurry up."

"You take the pie, and ride home on the trolley, and wait for me by my house, and I'll skate home."

She held out the pie to him, slowly, as if it would burn her hand to give it up. So Peter quickly dropped the nickel into her jacket pocket and skated away. He didn't look back, but as the trolley passed him, somebody was banging loudly on the window, and he looked up at Veronica, thumbing her nose at him as she passed.

He stuck out his tongue in return and felt happy and important. He'd certainly patched things up for Veronica. The day had ended a lot better than it had begun. It certainly was a good feeling knowing that you'd done something for a friend. Peter squared his shoulders and began skating in earnest. He had a long way to go. But how could she ever have thought he'd pass for a five-year-old. Nobody would ever take him for a five-year-old. Sometimes she could be an awful sap!

5

The annex of the high school that Peter went to lay on the other side of the park. All first, second, and third termers went to the annex.

It was a long walk from where Peter lived, and on rainy days, it was an exciting one. Everybody would arrive at school wet and wind-swept and full of high spirits. On rainy days, most teachers seemed to understand that serious work could not begin when the bell rang—that a period of distillation must be allowed before wet feet could be settled beneath desks, pink cheeks fade to a studious pallor, and giggles and squeals converted to the restrained response of "present" when the roll call was sounded.

On this rainy Monday, Peter's mother was still not talking to him, which made him uncomfortable, but which also meant that he was able to get out of the house without her telling him to wear his rubbers.

In the park, he caught sight of Veronica flopping

along ahead and he shouted for her to stop. Veronica never wore rubbers or carried an umbrella. She'd been wearing the same kind of rain outfit for as long as he'd known her, and he couldn't help snickering quickly to himself as he hurried up to her. It was a poncho, she said, left in her stepfather's cleaning store, a huge square of khaki-colored material that she had flung over her head. It covered her whole body, down to her ankles, and it kept her books and the rest of her dry. But she sure looked funny. When the wind whipped, as it did today, the corners of the poncho billowed out on all sides, making her look like a fat, funny version of Bat Man.

She twirled around a couple of times while she was waiting for him, and Peter got the impression that she must think she cut a pretty glamorous figure. It made him snicker again, but call out kindly, "Hi, Veronica. How was the pie?"

"O.K." Veronica's face grew thoughtful as the two of them fell into step. "But that Stanley—oh, is he a pest! He wouldn't eat any. He kept hiccuping all night, and my mother said it was my fault."

"Why was it your fault?" Peter yelled, as a gust of wind nearly blew off his hat.

"Oh, because I didn't take him along with me yesterday. Every time he doesn't get his way he hiccups. I can't stand him."

Veronica was always saying that Stanley was a pest and that she couldn't stand him, but just let anybody agree with her, as Peter well knew, and she was sure to fly off the handle. So he just held on to his hat and said nothing.

"Listen," said Veronica, "on Friday, when we go skating, suppose I come and pick you up instead of you coming to my house?"

The vision of his mother's cold eyes and tight mouth over this morning's breakfast table made him say quickly, "No, no! Let's meet someplace else."

"Where?"

"In front of the library."

"O.K."

Other rain-draped figures began to congeal on the path ahead.

"There's Bill," Peter said. "He's got my snake handbook. Let's catch up with him."

He hurried along, and it wasn't until he had nearly caught up with Bill that he realized Veronica had not followed along after him. He turned, and saw her billowing along a different path that led through the park. What a character! She'd never walk with the other kids if she could help it, only with him.

He hesitated but it was too late to catch up with her now, and besides, Bill had stopped and was waiting for him.

"Have you got my snake handbook?" he shouted.

"Yup, here it is." Bill handed him the book and the two of them hurried to catch up with the other kids. There were Paul Lucas, Frank Scacalossi, and Jeffrey Lobel walking about three feet behind a group of girls, and acting as if they were worlds apart. The boys were tussling with each other, splashing and snorting and watching the girls out of the corners of their eyes. Peter and Bill joined the boys. Jeffrey turned around when he saw Peter, and yelled, "Hi, stranger! Long time no see." Then he yanked Peter's hat off and began tossing it around to the other boys. Peter elbowed Bill in the ribs, stepped on Frank's foot, butted Jeffrey, and retrieved his hat from the puddle where it had landed. Then all of them paused for a moment to look at the girls.

There were only three of them—one in pink, one in yellow, and one in blue plaid. The one in blue plaid was the smallest one, and she was the one Peter looked at longest. That was Roslyn Gellert. Not that girls interested him much. Veronica didn't count as a girl. But if he had to give an opinion as to which girl was the least obnoxious in his class, he would have said Roslyn Gellert.

Last term, in eighth grade, his teacher had asked him to help Roslyn with her math. He had enjoyed watching the way her soft face wrinkled helplessly over the work, and the fact that her mother had given him milk and homemade doughnuts on the two occasions that they had studied at her house. She was not a particularly pretty girl or a particularly smart girl or even a girl much admired by the other boys. But she was the shortest girl in the class, a few inches shorter than he, and this final virtue, along with her others, made him think pleasant thoughts about her when he didn't have anything more important to think about.

The girls seemed impervious to the fact that there was anybody at all walking behind them. The one in pink had a pink umbrella that matched her raincoat, and she shifted it so that she could lean over and whisper something in the one in yellow's ear. Both of them began tittering.

"Can't stand that Lorraine Jacobs," said Frank. "She's the worst one of the bunch."

A sudden gust of wind blew the pink umbrella out of its owner's hand, and Frank bounded off in pursuit. The girls stopped and waited until he brought it back.

"Thanks, Frank," Lorraine said smoothly. Then she turned and smiled at all the boys. "Oh, hello there," she said, as if she were suddenly aware of them.

The two camps converged and stood with the rain pouring down on them, waiting.

Then Lorraine said, "I was going to ask all of you if you could come to a party at my house this Saturday night?"

"What kind of a party?" Paul asked suspiciously.

"Oh, not a birthday party," Lorraine said quickly, "just a party."

"Who's going to be there?" Peter asked, not looking at Roslyn.

"Linda, Frieda, Roslyn, Reba . . . some of the other kids . . . and me," she giggled. "And all of you, if you can come, and Marv Green. I want to ask him, and . . . oh, I don't know."

"What'll we do?" Bill asked.

"Gee, whatever we feel like," Lorraine said. "We can play games and maybe dance . . ."

"DANCE!"

"And we'll have refreshments. It'll start about seven-thirty and end about ten-thirty. Just let me know, will you?"

She and the other girls joined ranks again and began walking off. The boys huddled together behind.

"Parties are stupid," said Frank, looking at Lorraine's pink back. "I'm not going. Are you, Bill?"

"Naa. Are you, Peter?"

"Well," said Peter, watching Roslyn's red umbrella bob up and down, "I don't know. I'll go if Marv goes."

Paul said, "They're sappy, those parties. All they want to do is dance."

The other boys nodded. Peter had never been to an evening party with girls, and although he felt uncertain, he thought he might just try it this once, especially if Roslyn was going to be there.

"I'm not going to dance," said Bill, "but if there are refreshments, maybe I'll just look in for a little while, if Peter goes."

By the time they arrived at school, the boys had agreed to go, if only for the sake of the refreshments, but all of them had decided to meet first at Frank's

house and go together. Peter was pretty sure Marv
would go as long as he was going.

Peter's home-room teacher, Mr. Bailey, was very
popular with the boys and heartily disliked by the
girls. He walked with a cane, due to a wound he had
suffered in the First World War, over twenty years
ago. He had been a colonel in the American Army
in France, had received the Distinguished Service
Cross, and liked to reminisce. He was now an officer
in the Civil Defense, and had inspired some of the
boys in the class to go down to their local head-
quarters and volunteer as messengers. Every morning he liked to discuss the present war over in Eu-
rope with his class and analyze the rights and wrongs
in the strategy used by the Allies against Hitler. It
was only a matter of time, he said, before the United
States became involved in the war, and he, for one,
was ready. The boys enjoyed listening to him while
the girls usually kept looking at the clock. Except
for Veronica.

But it was not for his wound or his war stories
that the girls disliked him so. It was mainly because
he called them by their last names, the same way
he did with the boys. It was, "Jacobs, bring this
down to the office," and "Gellert, collect the permis-
sion slips," or "Kirby, sharpen the pencils." They
had waited a long time for high school where teachers were supposed to call them "Miss Jacobs," "Miss
Gellert," "Miss Kirby," and did, except for here, in
their own official room.

And if his lack of sensitivity over their names wasn't bad enough, his affection for low life was the final straw. Mr. Bailey taught science, and his room was filled with cases and cases of snakes. No stuffed squirrels or owls for him—like Mr. Gray, their old nature teacher in P. S. 63, used to display. All these snakes were live—thirty-seven of them. Mr. Bailey got a big kick out of the fact that this term he also had thirty-seven students in his class, and he proceeded to name each of the snakes by one of his students' names. At first, he suggested that each student feed and look after his own namesake, but the reaction had been so violent on the part of the girls—and some of the boys, too, for that matter—that Mr. Bailey had been forced to withdraw his suggestion and ask for volunteers. Five had volunteered —Bill Stover, Harold Jenkins, Ralph Crespi, Veronica Ganz, and Peter Wedemeyer. Since Peter's hand had gone up first, he was appointed captain of the snake squad, and along with his corpsmen, cleaned the cases and fed and watered their inhabitants.

On rainy days, when the students were unable to eat their lunches in the schoolyard (there being no lunchroom in the annex), all classes had to eat in their own home rooms. Problems arose when a number of girls objected to eating their lunches while many of the snakes were eating theirs. Lorraine Jacobs, one day, had put up a book in front of the case adjacent to her seat, to cut off the view of her neighbor who was not quite finished digesting his

meal of kicking frog legs. Mr. Bailey had accused
her of cruelty to animals, and although she murmured under her breath about cruelty to humans,
she still had to take down the book and skip lunch
for the day.

Mr. Bailey was entertaining them with incidents
involved in the rout of Verdun when Veroncia, who
was putting water in some of the cages, cried out
suddenly, "Mr. Bailey, Mr. Bailey, he's dead!"

Mr. Bailey grabbed his cane and heaved himself
up to his feet. "What's that, Ganz? Who's dead?"

"It's Ralph Peterson. He's not moving. Oh, I think
he's dead."

Everybody looked at Ralph Peterson, the boy, who
smiled nervously. Mr. Bailey hurried to the back of
the room, pulled the snake out, and inspected it.
Everybody could see how it hung limp and unmov-
ing from his hand.

"He's dead, all right," Mr. Bailey said bitterly,
"and he was the best one of the bunch." He peered
into the cage and shouted, "Just look at this mess
in here, Ganz! The whole floor is full of water. I
told you a million times, their cages had to be dry."

Veronica blinked and looked helplessly at Peter.
But she said nothing while Mr. Bailey continued to
berate her. When he had finished and waved her
away with his hand, she slowly sat down at her seat
and suddenly sunk her head in her hands.

Peter stood up quickly and said, "Mr. Bailey!"

"What is it, Wedemeyer?"

"It's just that Veronica wasn't responsible for taking care of Ralph Peterson's cage. All of us on the squad divided up the cages, and Ralph Peterson's was Harold Jenkins. But you know he was sick last week—I mean Harold Jenkins—and I thought I had remembered to look after all his snakes but I guess I hadn't."

"That doesn't make any difference," said Mr. Bailey unfeelingly. "The snake's dead, and your squad just wasn't on the ball. Make sure it doesn't happen again, Wedemeyer, or I'll have to appoint a new squad."

"Yes, sir," said Peter, sitting down. He tried to catch Veronica's eye, but her face was still buried in her hands.

When the bell rang for the students to go to their first class, Lorraine and some of the other girls surrounded Veronica in the hall, and cooed sympathetically about the injustice that had been done. Peter hurried up, too, and heard Veronica say sadly, "He just didn't realize it wasn't me, and the snake was a beauty."

"Well," said Lorraine, "don't you feel bad about it. It wasn't your fault."

Veronica nodded but she still looked unhappy. Lorraine reached out and put an arm on her shoulder and said suddenly, "Say, would you like to come to a party I'm giving this Saturday night?"

That Lorraine Jacobs wasn't really such a bad egg, after all, Peter thought. He smiled encouragingly at

Veronica, who suddenly had a frantic look in her eye
and seemed even more unhappy.

"Party?" she said. "What kind of party?"

"Oh, not a birthday party," said Lorraine, "just a
party. A lot of kids in the class will be there. I
hope you can make it too."

When Peter arrived home from school that afternoon, his mother was sewing something on the sewing machine.

"Hi, Ma," he yelled, as he came through the door.

No answer.

He came up behind her and gave her a quick peck
on her cheek. She stopped sewing and looked at
him coldly. "So what do you want?" she said.

"Oh, Ma," Peter said, "don't be like that."

She resumed sewing, and Peter stood there trying
to think of some topic of conversation that might
make her happy.

"Ma," he said, "I'm going to a party, Saturday
night."

The sewing machine stopped whirring. "What kind
of a party?" she said suspiciously.

"Oh, not a birthday party," he said quickly. "It
won't cost anything to go."

"I don't mean that," she said. "Who's giving the
party?"

"Lorraine Jacobs."

"Oh," said his mother, moving her chair back and
looking at him with a look that was not quite so

cool, "Rose Jacob's girl—a nice girl. Who else is going?"

"Mary Green and Roslyn Gellert and Paul Lucas . . ." Peter named some of the children he knew
his mother approved of.

"And . . . anybody else?"

"I guess so. I don't know all the kids she's asking."

"She's a smart girl," his mother said comfortably.
"She'll know whom to invite. I don't have to worry
about her. What time is the party?"

"Seven-thirty to ten-thirty."

"All right. I'll tell Papa to come and get you at
ten-thirty."

Peter yelled, "I don't want Papa to come and get
me. I'm not a baby any more. Don't you dare tell
Papa to come and get me. It's just a block away.
I know the way home."

"All right, all right. He can stand on the corner."

"If I see him standing on the corner," Peter said
between his teeth, "I'll go the other way."

Mrs. Wedemeyer suddenly began to laugh. She
pulled him into her lap and stroked his hair and
kissed him, and he let her do it because of the way
she had cried yesterday. But it wasn't easy, and he
certainly wished she'd stop treating him like a five-
year-old.

6

When she still hadn't arrived by four-thirty, Peter decided she wasn't coming. Once more he skated up to the corner to look for her, and sure enough, this time he saw her skating across 169th Street. Somebody was with her, or more accurately stated, somebody was following along behind her. It was Stanley.

"If she thinks," Peter muttered to himself, "that that kid's going to tag along after us, she's got another think coming."

"Gee whizz," he shouted to her as she drew closer, "I'm freezing to death waiting for you. What took you so long?"

Veronica's face was grim. "Him," she said, motioning behind her. "Mary Rose can go off with her friends and that's O.K. But not me. My mother's at the store, and he doesn't want to stay there, so she said I've got to take him along."

Stanley came hurrying up, and Veronica said, "You keep away from me. I can't stand you."

"O.K., Veronica," Stanley said meekly, and leaned against a hydrant and made a face at Peter.

Veronica flopped down angrily on the library steps and grumbled down at the skates on her feet. "I told her just on Friday. Let me off the hook on Friday. The other days I don't mind. But no, she said I have to take him, and that you—well, never mind about that."

Stanley pulled something out of his pocket and called, "Veronica, you want a piece of gum?"

"Shut up, you, or I'll . . ." Veronica shook her fist, and Stanley looked at her with such a happy, adoring look that Veronica's fist dropped into her lap, and she turned away her face and muttered helplessly, "One of these days, you'll see what I'll do. One of these days . . ."

"Gee," Peter said, "I figured we'd skate down to the river today and ride back on the el. I even have ten cents. I was going to treat you."

"O.K.," Stanley said. "Let's go to the river."

"Not you!" Veronica shouted. "We can't go anywhere with you along."

"So let's go home, Veronica. That's O.K. with me too."

"Listen," Peter said in her ear, "did you try to get him to go and stay in your parents' store?"

"What do you think took me so long? I've been talking myself blue in the face but he won't go."

"Did you offer him something?"

"Like what?"

"You know," Peter whispered, cupping his hands around his mouth. "Bribe him with something he likes. He's only a little kid. Offer him something he's dying for if he'll stay in the store."

Veronica drew back her head and looked thoughtfully at Peter. Then she nodded.

"Stanley," she said in a sweet voice, "come here, Stanley."

Stanley approached carefully.

"That's all right, Stanley. I'm not going to hit you. Come on, that's a boy. Here, sit down next to me."

Stanley sat down.

"Look, Stanley, how about this? You stay at the store this afternoon with Mama and Ralph, and tomorrow I'll take you any place you want to go."

"Where?" asked Stanley.

"That's up to you," said Veronica, smiling. "Any place *you* like."

"Any place?"

"Uh, huh."

Stanley considered for a moment. Then he said eagerly, "Could we ride the double-decker bus?"

"Sure," Veronica said agreeably. "We'll take the train downtown and ride the buses."

"Not the closed double-decker buses," said Stanley. "The kind that's open on top.

"Sure."

"And I can sit in the front?"

"Wherever you like."

"And just you and me?"

"Uh, huh."

"Nobody else? Not him?" motioning to Peter.

"Just us. Maybe Mary Rose, if she wants to come."

"No, not Mary Rose. Just us."

"O.K., just us."

"Back and forth. Not just one ride?"

"For as long as you like."

"You swear to God?"

"I swear to God." Veronica crossed her heart. "Cross my heart and hope to die." She stood up and held out her hand to him. "Come on."

"Where are we going?"

"I'm taking you over to the store."

"I don't want to go to the store."

"But you just said if I take you riding on the double-decker bus tomorrow, you'll stay in the store today."

"No, I didn't," cried Stanley, and he began to hiccup. "I just said I want to ride the bus tomorrow, and you swore to God that you'd take me."

Veronica reached out a curling hand for him, and he scurried away from the steps back to the hydrant.

"You—hic—promised," he cried indignantly.

"You see how he is," Veronica said helplessly to Peter. And she sat down again on the library steps. "You just can't even talk to him."

"Let me try," Peter whispered.

He skated over toward Stanley, and Stanley retreated around the far side of the hydrant.

"Don't be afraid, Stanley," Peter said kindly. "I just want to talk to you."

"I don't want to talk to you."

"Stanley," Peter said persuasively, feeling in his pocket, "how would you like a Coke?"

Stanley kept moving around the hydrant, his eyes filled with hatred.

"If you go to the store," Peter said, "I'll give you a nickel and you can buy a Coke."

"I won't!" Stanley shouted.

"A dime?" Peter suggested. So they wouldn't ride home on the train.

"No!"

"Let's see," Peter said, still not discouraged. He dug down in his pocket and began emptying its contents.

"Look, Stanley," he said, "I've got these beautiful stamps from France—three of them. Look! This one's green and this one's blue and here—look at this beautiful orange one. And you can have all three."

"No!"

"Hey, look what I've got," Peter said enthusiastically, drawing out a small square mirror. He held it in the sunlight and let the reflection flash against the library building, the stairs, over Veronica's skates, up the hydrant, and finally right in Stanley's face.

Stanley blinked, licked his lips, looked hungrily at the mirror, and whispered, "No!"

Peter dug down to the very bottom of his pocket, pulled out his house key, and fished out a couple of pencils that lay underneath.

"See, Stanley, this one's a red pencil, and this one says, KATZ'S LUMBERYARD on it, and the eraser's not even used. You can have them both, and . . ."

"What's that?" Stanley said, pointing.

"What's what?" Peter followed Stanley's pointed finger. "Oh, that's just my key." The key was attached to a chain that also held a blue rabbit's foot. Peter said, his eyes narrowing, "You want to hold the rabbit's foot? Here, hold it. It brings you good luck."

He held out the chain, and Stanley took it and rubbed the rabbit's foot and said, "It's soft."

"Tell you what," said Peter, the end plainly in sight. "I'll give you the rabbit's foot if you stay in the store."

Stanley hicced and continued stroking.

"And you can have the mirror too."

Veronica stood up. "And tomorrow I'll take you riding on the buses."

"Here, give me the chain, and I'll take off the rabbit's foot for you."

Stanley jiggled the rabbit's foot on the chain. "I like the chain too," he said.

"O.K., O.K., you can have the chain too. Just let me take my key off."

"I like the key too," Stanley said.

"But it's the key to my house. You don't need the key to my house."

"I like the key," Stanley said stubbornly.

Peter sighed. What a crazy kid! But all right, let him keep the key then. He could always have another key made for himself.

Veronica was watching him and he said, "All right, keep the whole thing. Now let's go!"

"Where?" said Stanley.

"To the store," Veronica shouted.

Stanley rubbed the rabbit's foot once more, then he twirled the chain in his hand, and flung it as far as he could into the street.

"I won't!" he cried.

By the time Peter had retrieved his key, and been nearly knocked over by several cars and trucks, Stanley had fled halfway up the block, and Veronica was standing up looking after him.

"I don't know what's gotten into him lately," she said thoughtfully. "He never used to be like this."

"Well you just let me know when you find out," Peter said angrily. "I've wasted enough time with that brat, and that's all for today. Good-by!"

"Good-by, Peter," Veronica said meekly.

He began skating away, but she called after him anxiously, "Peter!"

"What?" over his shoulder, still skating.

"Next Friday, I swear, Peter, I'll come by myself. O.K.?"

Peter slowed down and turned around. Veronica

stood looking at him, and behind her, half a block beyond, Stanley stood watching too.

So the day was wasted anyway. Even if he did go off by himself, where was he going to go? Home? And his mother would ask him where he'd been and who was he with. Mothers! And that reminded him of something Veronica had said, and something that he wanted to ask her. Slowly he skated back and sat down again on the library steps.

"Aren't you going home?" she said.

"No." He looked at her and wondered how to ask.

"Peter," she said hesitantly, "can I ask you something?"

"What?"

She sat down next to him and said carefully, "This party tomorrow night—are you going?"

"I guess so. Aren't you?"

"No."

"Why not?"

She shook her head. "I've never been to that kind of a party before. I don't think I'd like it."

"Well, neither have I. But you know all the kids. Come on."

She looked away and said, "Well, if I did go— and I'm not—but if I did, could I go with you?"

"Sure, if you like. But I'm going with all the fellows. We're going to meet at Frank Scacalossi's house and we're going to go together. You can meet us there."

Veronica said, "I don't think I'm going to go."

"Well, why not?" Peter said impatiently.

"Because," Veronica said quickly, "I think she only invited me because she was sorry for me. She's a nice girl, that Lorraine, and I never had any trouble with her, but I think it was really because of the snake. I mean, I don't think she would have invited me otherwise, and I don't really know the girls so well."

"You know the boys," said Peter.

"Yeah." She and Peter grinned at each other, remembering those days back in P. S. 63 when each of the boys had fallen under the weight of Veronica's fists.

Peter caught a glimpse of Stanley inching his way back up the street. "Just meet us over at Frank's house at twenty minutes after seven. O.K.?"

"I don't know."

"Anyway, now I want to ask you something."

"What?"

Stanley reached the hydrant and balanced himself carefully against it, his eyes, full of loathing, on Peter.

"What did your mother say?" There now, he'd asked it.

"I told you. She said I had to watch Stanley."

"No, I mean what did she say about me?"

"Oh—well—she doesn't know you too well. She only met you a couple of times, and . . ."

"She doesn't like me, right?"

"Well . . ."

"Why doesn't she like me?"

Veronica said evasively, "You know how it is. She thinks a big girl like me shouldn't go around with a boy, and—well—it doesn't matter. I'm old enough to do what I like."

Peter took a deep breath. "Does she mind because I'm Jewish?"

"Aw, Peter!" Veronica's face was strained.

"Come on, tell me, because my mother minds that you're not Jewish."

"Honestly?" Veronica brightened. "Gee, that's great, because my mother does mind that you are Jewish. I'm so glad. I was so ashamed. I wasn't going to tell you."

They grinned at each other. Veronica said happily, "Maybe I will go to the party tomorrow. What time was that you're meeting at Frank's house?"

"Seven-twenty." Peter stood up. "Come on."

"Where?"

"Let's skate. We'll go over to the park."

"And Stanley?"

"We'll ignore him."

"Yaah!" yelled Stanley.

"But he won't ignore us," said Veronica.

"Who cares?" said Peter. He felt as if a weight had been lifted off his chest. His mother, her mother, Stanley, the whole world—nobody was going to stop him from going skating with his friend on Friday afternoon. Just let them try!

7

"Here?" Bill Stover said. "You told her to come here? Are you crazy or something?"

There were six of them—Peter, Marv, Frank, Paul, Jeffrey, and Bill standing in front of Frank's house ready to embark.

Paul sniffed the air around Jeffrey and said, "What's that stuff you got on your hair? It smells like Flit."

"It is Flit," Frank said. "It's supposed to keep bedbugs and girls away."

"Aw, cut it out," said Jeffrey, passing a hand over his head. "It's just the stuff my father uses."

"Your father's bald," said Paul.

"So how come you had to tell her to come here?" Bill said again. "Who needs her?"

"It's a free country," Peter said testily, wondering where she was anyway. It must be past seven-thirty. "I can ask anybody I like."

"How come you're not wearing a tie?" Frank said to Marv. "You look like you've just come from the coal mines."

Marv fingered the collar of his plaid flannel shirt and said meekly, "I didn't know we were supposed to wear ties. It's not school."

"It's going to look just great," Bill continued, "the six of us marching up to Lorraine's house with her. What'll they think?"

"Look, what are you getting all steamed up about?" Frank said, taking off his tie and putting it in his pocket. "It's not like it was Lorraine or one of those drippy girls. It's only Veronica."

"I can't stand her," Bill said. "If I'd known she was coming I would have stayed home."

"Well, it's not too late now," Peter said, waving his arm in the direction of Bill's house. "Why don't you go home. You'd never be missed."

"You're really getting nutty," Bill shouted. "She's really turning you into a first-class nut. All of a sudden you're so palsy-walsy with her. It's crazy! Last term you couldn't stand her and this term you follow her like a sappy shadow."

Marv said, looking at Frank's pocket, "If you're not going to wear that tie, could you lend it to me?"

"That's gratitude," said Frank. "I took it off because I didn't want you to be the only one not wearing a tie."

"Let's all not wear ties," said Jeffrey, pulling his off.

"You take that back!" Peter said, clenching his fists, and moving in on Bill.

"Come on, come on, break it up!" Frank said, handing Marv the tie. "I'll go up and get another tie, and if she's still not here by the time I get back, we'll go without her."

"You mean we're going to wear them?" said Jeffrey, fishing his tie out of his pocket and looking at it mournfully.

Veronica still hadn't come by the time Frank returned with another tie, so the pack of them began walking slowly in the direction of Lorraine's house. She must have changed her mind about coming, Peter guessed, and wondered why she always seemed to avoid the other kids. One of these days he'd ask her. But wasn't it funny how everything had changed in six months' time. Why, back in P. S. 63, everybody was scared of Veronica. People would go in the other direction when they saw her coming. They hated her and grumbled about her all the time. But now that they were in high school, and she'd stopped fighting, she was the one who went in the other direction. Why? Some of the kids laughed at her, and he guessed she didn't like that. He didn't like it either. But nobody really hated her any more —nobody except Bill.

Peter felt uncomfortable when he thought about Bill. Because it was his fault, really. He had worked out the plan for a gang up on Veronica last term and had drawn Bill and Paul into it. He had been to blame for the whole thing, and yet once it was over, he and Veronica were friends, Paul had laughed and forgotten, but Bill still brooded. Somehow it didn't seem fair that Bill, who had been the most unwilling to take part in the gang up, should end up still smarting over it.

Anyway, Veronica was evidently not coming tonight. He felt a little annoyed at her because if she'd only said she wasn't coming in the first place, he wouldn't have had that argument with Bill. But maybe it was just as well that she wasn't coming. He had other things to worry about tonight, like what do you do at a party with girls? And would Roslyn Gellert be there? And if she was, would she think he looked as handsome as his mother said he did? And would his father be waiting outside for him even though he promised he wouldn't?

"Well, what do we do after it's over?" Jeffrey said urgently, as they paused before going up the stairs of Lorraine's house.

"What do you mean?" said Bill.

"My mother said you have to take them home."

"Why?" said Marv. "They know how to get home themselves."

"No, he's right," said Frank. "A boy is supposed to take a girl home after a party at night."

"I'll take Lorraine home," Paul said, grinning.

"That's not fair," said Frank.

"Why not? You always say you hate her the most."

"It has nothing to do with that," shouted Frank. "It's because she lives here."

"Who are you going to take home, Peter?" said Jeffrey.

"I don't know," Peter said, knowing whom he'd like to take. "Who are you?"

"I don't know. How about you, Bill?"

"I don't know."

"Me, neither."

"You, Marv?"

"How should I know."

When they finally made it up the stairs, Lorraine opened the door for them and said brightly, "Hi— you're late. Come on in."

They could hear the sound of music coming from the living room down at the end of the hall. As they passed the kitchen, Mrs. Jacobs looked out and smiled and nodded at them.

"Oh, Marvin," she said, coming through the door, and walking along with them, "how's your papa?"

"He's better, Mrs. Jacobs," said Marv.

"Is he back to work?"

"Not yet but the doctor thinks maybe in another week or so."

"I'm glad. And how's your mama?"

"She's fine. Thanks."

They reached the living room and saw that the girls had already arrived. Most of them were sitting around the room deep in conversation. A record was playing on the record player, and Roba and Frieda were dancing a Lindy Hop.

"I felt so bad when I heard he was sick again," Mrs. Jacobs continued. "Tell your parents I'll be over tomorrow to see them."

"Ma—please!" Lorraine said urgently.

"What? Oh—all right, I'm going. Have a nice time, children." Mrs. Jacobs moved back through the hall to the kitchen, and the boys stood at the entrance to the room, waiting.

"Why don't you drop your coats on the bed in there," Lorraine said, pointing to the bedroom on the other side of the French doors, "and then we can start."

Peter caught a glimpse of himself in the mirror over the dresser, after he had laid his coat on the bed. Hair smooth on his head, nice suit, new tie— he looked, well, he guessed he looked all right. He waited until all the other boys were ready, and together they moved back through the door into the room.

He knew that Roslyn was sitting on the couch. He'd seen her as soon as he came in. She had a pink sweater on and pearls. All the girls were wearing sweaters and pearls. Now, he figured, she'd look up and smile at him. He'd smile at her. She'd move over a little bit on the couch. He'd walk over and sit down next to her. She'd say, "You look nice, Peter." He'd say, "So do you." Then she'd say . . .

But she didn't look up. Nobody looked up and all the boys remained together near the French doors.

"Well, I guess we can start," Lorraine said. "Everybody's here except Veronica. Maybe she couldn't come."

"Good riddance to bad rubbish," said Bill. Peter tightened his fists, but then Frieda giggled and said, "You're some wit, Bill, a regular half-wit."

The girls tittered, and Bill squared his shoulders and said, "Oh, yeah!" Then he broke from the ranks, walked over to the chair where Frieda was sitting, and made believe he was going to sit down on top of her. She squealed, and after a while Bill settled down on the arm of her chair. So that was one down.

"Well now," Lorraine said, looking with satisfaction at Frieda and Bill, "what should we do?"

"Eat," said Paul, and he walked over to the bridge table in one corner of the room and inspected the platters of potato chips, cookies, and pretzel sticks. Two down.

"How about a game?" said Lorraine.

"Let's play Coffee Pot," suggested Linda.

"Naa!" in a chorus from the boys.

"How about Indian Chief?"

"Naa!"

"Charades?"

"That sappy game!"

"So what do you want to play?"

"Stickball," said Frank.

And Lorraine said, "Just for that, mister, you're

going to help me carry in the drinks for everybody. Come on!"

Frank made a face, but he didn't struggle when Lorraine took his arm and pulled him along with her to the kitchen. Three down. And that left Peter, Jeffrey, and Marv standing at their post.

Marv said, looking at the record player, "That's a new portable. I think the speaker's in the top." He ambled off, and that was four down.

Jeffrey whispered nervously, "Does it really smell like Flit?"

"What?"

"The stuff on my hair."

Peter took a furtive sniff and said, "Yeah."

"Where's the bathroom?"

"Up the hall."

Jeffrey groaned and hurried out of the room. And that was five gone. Peter looked at Roslyn. She was still talking to Reba on the couch, and he decided what he'd do is walk over to the refreshment table, take a handful of chips, and sort of casually pass in front of the couch. She'd look up, and he'd say, "Care for some potato chips?"

He had just arrived at the table when Lorraine and Frank returned with the bottles of soda pop, and then there was a mild crush while all the kids converged on the table to make their selection.

Everybody seemed to feel more convivial with a bottle of pop in his or her hand, and they played Coffee Pot for a while. Peter ended up sitting next to Jeffrey on one side and Linda on the other. After they got tired of playing Coffee Pot, they played Indian Chief and Charades and a couple of other games. Then Lorraine suggested that they dance.

"We're a girl short." Linda offered the interesting statistic. "Since Veronica didn't come, that makes five girls and six boys."

"Somebody has to dance with the broom," Reba giggled.

"Me!"

"Me!"

"Me!"

"Me!"

"Me!"

"Me!" shouted the six boys, and there was a mad scramble for the kitchen.

Mr. Jacobs was reading his paper at the table when they all galloped in, and he said, "What's going on?"

"It's O.K., Papa," Lorraine said, hurrying in. "We need the broom."

Mr. Jacobs looked meaningfully at the clock over the refrigerator and then at his daughter. "It's nine-thirty, Lorraine," he said.

"Pa, please," Lorraine said. "Come on, boys, let's go back."

Paul had the broom and began cavorting around with it. Lorraine put a record on and she and Frank began dancing. So that made two couples dancing. Lorraine and Frank, and Paul and the broom. Peter looked at Roslyn again. If she'd only look up, he'd walk right over and ask her to dance. He was beginning to feel desperate. The evening was slipping by, and she hadn't even noticed him. What was the matter with her anyway? Or was there something the matter with him? Maybe something was wrong with him. Something *must* be wrong with him.

"Where is it?" he whispered to Jeffrey.

"What?"

"The bathroom."

"Up the hall."

Peter hurried into the bathroom, locked the door, and carefully examined his face in the mirror. There was a red blotch on his chin, and he'd never noticed before but his left eye was definitely larger than his right eye. He looked awful. Carefully he stood up on the bathtub so he could get a glimpse of the rest of himself in the mirror above the sink. The suit didn't fit right. The shoulders were too big and the pants were too long. What a mess!

Grimly he walked back out into the hall and wondered if he should go home. He was having a miserable time.

Voices emanated from the kitchen as he approached. Mr. Jacobs was saying plaintively, "But I want to go to bed. I worked hard all day and I'm falling off my feet."

"A little longer, Max. Don't be like that. It's nearly ten. Another half hour, it'll be over. Don't you want her to have a good time?"

"In the day," Mr. Jacobs moaned. "Can't she have a good time in the day?"

"Shh, someone's outside. Hello," Mrs. Jacobs said, sticking her head out into the hall. "Oh, Peter." She said nodding agreeably. "Are you having a good time?"

"Great!" Peter said glumly, walking slowly back to the living room.

Roslyn was dancing with Reba, and Lorraine and Frank were dancing too. Bill was talking to Frieda, Marv was busy at the record player, and Linda was chatting away to Paul over the platters of potato chips and pretzels. Jeffrey was standing near the French doors. "Even I can smell it now," Jeffrey said. "Maybe it was the Flit."

Peter glared at Roslyn and Reba. He'd try once more and that was it. But how? You couldn't just go up to two girls dancing together and cut in on one of them. How come girls could dance together anyway but boys couldn't? Besides, he didn't know how to dance so even if he did cut in, what then?

He looked over at the empty couch, and an idea born of desperation grew in his mind. He crossed the room, sat down in the middle of the empty couch, and waited. After a while the dance ended, and the two girls returned to the couch.

Now was the time for him to look at Roslyn and say something clever. The girls stood there waiting. Peter concentrated, but he couldn't think of anything clever to say. As a matter of fact, he couldn't think

of anything to say at all. So he moved over. Reba sat down next to him and Roslyn next to her. The two of them began yakking again.

The doorbell rang twice, and Roslyn rose and said to Lorraine, "That's my father. He said he'd pick me up at ten."

She hurried into the bedroom, returned with her coat, said, "Good-by everybody," and left.

After she had gone, Reba turned to Peter and said, "What happened to Veronica?"

"I don't know," Peter said, wondering if he should go home or eat some potato chips first. "I guess she just decided not to come."

"Oh!" Reba's plump face looked full of mysterious wisdom. "We thought maybe she was coming later, and that's why you were standing around—sort of waiting for her."

"I wasn't waiting for anybody," Peter protested. "There wasn't anything to do, and I was just waiting for something to happen."

"Oh—well Roslyn thought you were waiting for Veronica."

"Why should she think I was waiting for Veronica?" Peter snapped. "That's pretty stupid of her."

"I'll tell her." Reba giggled, and Peter looked at her with fury.

"Why should anybody think I was waiting for Veronica?" he repeated angrily.

Reba continued to giggle, so he stood up and said with dignity, "I'm going home."

"I guess I will too," Reba said, also standing up.

"Are you going now, Peter?" Jeffrey said eagerly. "I'm going too."

So the three of them left together, but when they got downstairs, Jeffrey, who lived over on Cottage Avenue, went off in the other direction, which meant that Peter ended up walking Reba home.

And that was the worst part of it. Even worse than arriving home and having to fend off his mother's questions. Alone in his bedroom finally, he thought angrily about what a bust the party had been. So Roslyn had avoided him because of Veronica. Well, that was her hard luck. She could flunk math for all he cared. Just let her come and ask him for help. Just let her. He'd be the one to look off vaguely into nowhere. And Bill—one more crack from Bill, and he'd pop him one in the mouth.

He tore off his tie, threw his jacket on the floor, and fished his skates out of the closet. Tomorrow morning, he'd go find Veronica and go skating in spite of all of them.

8

"What's the matter with you kids? Don't you have any respect for the dead?"

They hadn't noticed the man as they came skating up the path and they jumped as he stood up. He was holding a small gardening tool in his hand and had been planting something around one of the graves.

He motioned angrily toward their skates, and Veronica whispered, "Let's get out of here."

"You don't come into a cemetery with skates on," the man continued. "That's not right. That's not right at all. And what are you doing here anyway?"

Peter said uncomfortably, "We were just skating around Bronx Park and then we ended up here. We never saw this place before and so we thought we'd just come in and take a look, and—well—gee, Mister, I guess we weren't thinking. We'll take them off. I've never been in a cemetery before," he added lamely.

The man just stood there shaking his head back and forth. Peter sat down in the path and quickly unstrapped his skates. After a second, Veronica did the same. But the man kept standing there, looking at them. He didn't say anything, just watched them. Peter's skates clanged together when he stood up, holding them in one hand, and he separated them nervously, and one of them dropped, making a loud sound on the pavement.

The man's face bunched up then, and tears ran down his cheeks.

"Aw, Mister," Peter said, "We'll go now. We didn't mean anything."

The man tried to say something but his words caught in his throat, and he motioned with his hand toward the gravestone he was standing next to.

Veronica was the first to move. She walked around the man, and looked at the front of the stone. Peter followed her. The inscription on it said:

MARTIN FRANKLIN
1932–1940

and under that, in smaller letters:

OUR DEAR SON

The man said, "I told him that last time he was sick, I promised him a pair of skates with ball bearings, and I promised him a boat he could sail, and a pair of boxing gloves. He always wanted boxing gloves."

"Did he fight a lot?" Veronica asked curiously, and Peter looked at her in surprise. What a crazy question to ask. You never talked like that about dead people. Anytime the grownups in his family spoke about the dead, it was only in the most glowing terms. She should know better than to ask a question like that.

The man didn't seem to mind though. He smiled and said, "Oh, he was a real boy, my Martin. He got into lots of scrapes. He could lick any kid on the block. His mother didn't like it, but I knew he'd be all right. You don't want a boy to be a sissy."

"He must have been a wonderful boy," Peter said respectfully, but Veronica asked, "Did he get in trouble in school?"

The man hesitated, and Peter tried to catch Veronica's eye, and signal her to stop asking such foolish questions.

"Well," the man said slowly, "he didn't like school much. But he wasn't a bad boy—just a little lively. He had this old, crabby teacher who kept calling my wife into school all the time."

"Did you ever hit him?" Veronica asked.

"No, no," the man protested, "I never did." He shook his head a few times and then he swallowed, looked at Veronica, and said, "Sometimes. I had to. What do you do when a kid gets out of hand? If

I'd only known—but he was so big and strong. How could I know?"

"Sure," Veronica said easily, and then she put her skates down on one side of the grave and said, "What are you doing now?"

"Oh!" The man looked down at the little shovel in his hand. "I'm putting some new plants in, and then I'll weed and pull up the grass. I like to keep it looking nice."

Veronica crouched down over the grave. "Which ones are the weeds?"

"Those tall ones that stick up," said the man, and Veronica began pulling them out.

"Here, I'll help too," Peter said, putting his skates down and bending over another part of the small plot. He pulled out a few weeds, and then the man, Mr. Franklin, said, "No, not that one. That's a plant." He crouched down next to Peter and showed him the difference. "It's funny," he said, "but I never knew anything about plants or flowers. All my life I've lived in apartment houses. But since he's gone, I've been going around to the nurseries and learning. See that." He pointed to a spindly bush on one side of the grave. "That's an American Beauty rosebush. I planted it last time I was here. Next year, it'll bloom."

"Very nice," Peter said politely, but Veronica looked at the bush and said, "Where's your wife?"

"She's home. We've got a baby now—Katherine.

She was born a few months after Martin went, and there's Kenny and Jamie too. They're five and seven."

"Do they remember him?" Veronica asked.

"We don't talk about him much. My wife doesn't want them to feel bad. He's only been gone a little over a year, and I think maybe Kenny doesn't remember him any more, but I guess Jamie does. They used to play together a lot."

Veronica sat back, and her face was thoughtful. "If I was dead," she said, "I'd hate for nobody to remember me."

"I tell her that all the time," Mr. Franklin said eagerly, "but she says they're only kids and it'll upset them."

"If I was dead," Veronica went on, looking at the rosebush, "I'd want people to talk about me. I'd want them to get up in the morning, and when they sat down to eat breakfast, somebody'd say, 'There's the bowl Veronica ate her Rice Krispies out of.' And maybe somebody would say how I hated eggs. And they'd talk about me, and I wouldn't mind if Mary Rose or somebody said things that weren't so nice about me, as long as they kept talking and thinking about me. And I'd want them all to come out to the cemetery and to look at my grave, and maybe plant things and sit around and talk so I wouldn't be lonely."

"If you were dead, you wouldn't be lonely," Peter said.

IN
Memory of
JOHN EVENS

who died
April 29th 1836.
aged 50 years.
2 months, 13 days.

"How do you know?"

"Well," Mr. Franklin said unhappily, "none of them—the children I mean—has been here. When they're older, my wife says she'll take them."

"She's right," Peter said. "They're only little kids. Little kids shouldn't have to think about sad things like this. They should play and be happy. You have to protect little kids."

"But what about the little kid who's dead?" Veronica cried. "What about Martin?"

Mr. Franklin said gently, "It's not like we've forgotten him. Don't think that. My wife and I talk about him and think about him all the time. We'll never forget him. Don't think that." He put an arm out and pressed Veronica's shoulder as if he was comforting her, and she nodded and began pulling up weeds again.

When they were finished, Mr. Franklin offered them some money for helping but they both refused. Veronica said slowly, "Could I come here sometimes, even if you're not here, and weed? Would that be all right?"

Mr. Franklin didn't answer her question. He just said quickly, "I'm sorry about the skates. You go ahead and put them on." And then he hurried away.

"I'm not going to put them on. Are you?" Peter asked.

Veronica shook her head. Then she turned away and said, "If I was dead, would you forget about me?"

"What kind of stupid question is that?" Peter said uncomfortably. "You're not going to be dead."

"Someday I will."

"Not for a long time. Gee, why are you thinking about dying? Let's get out of here."

"But if I did die. Say I got hit by a truck or got polio, would you forget me?"

"But you're not going to die."

"But if I did. Would you?"

"Would I what?"

"You know—forget me."

"No," Peter said, "I wouldn't forget you. Now, let's go."

Veronica looked at him then and she said, "Peter, if you die, I swear, I'll never forget you. I'll talk about you all the time. I'll tell people how you used to wear a blue sweater and how smart you were in school. And I'll come all the time to where your grave is and I'll plant lots of rosebushes and take care of them." She clenched her fists. "I won't let anybody forget you. When you care for somebody it doesn't stop when he's dead. I won't let it. Ralph Peterson, the snake, he's dead, and Mr. Bailey threw him out in the garbage, but I'm not forgetting him. And you know what I'm going to do? Every day when I take care of my snakes, I'm going to tell them about Ralph Peterson. I'm going to whisper to them about how smart he used to be, and about that long white stripe he had down his back. I'm going to remind them. And I'd do the same for you, Peter, only more. So swear, if I die, you won't forget me either. Go on, swear on his grave!"

She put her hand on Martin Franklin's tombstone, and Peter looked at her wild face and thought, I mustn't laugh, I mustn't laugh.

So he put his hand on Martin Franklin's tombstone too, and he said, "I swear to God I'll never forget Veronica Ganz if she dies. And if I do, may I fall down dead!"

"And I swear," said Veronica fiercely, "that if Peter Wedemeyer dies first, I'll remember him and make everybody else remember him or may I be struck down dead!"

And then they were strolling along through the cemetery, carrying their skates over their shoulders, as if nothing important had happened. They began looking at the inscriptions on the other tombstones.

"Hey look at this one," Veronica shouted. "It's for a lady—Martha Prendergast, 1856–1932.

> If heaven is the reward for a life
> Passed in innocence and usefulness
> Then she was a favored candidate

Veronica read slowly. "I'll bet she was nice."

"Listen to this one," Peter said, bending over a very old, weathered stone. "It's another lady, Sarah T. Carey, 1806–1847.

Behold my friends as you pass by
As you are now, so once was I
As I am now, so you must be
Prepare for death and follow me

Brr! That's not very cheerful, is it?"

"What do you think of this one?" Veronica cried. "It's a man, Matthew Lukes, 1850–1903.

To live in hearts
We leave behind
Is not to die

That's beautiful." She sat down next to the tombstone and began pulling weeds. There were many of them, and Peter, watching her, suddenly began chuckling. "I see you've got a new occupation."

"Oh, shut up!"

Peter moved off and began inspecting some of the other stones.

"Peter!"

"What?"

"Did you ever think about what you'd like them to write on your tombstone?"

"No—did you?"

"No—but I'm thinking now."

Peter looked at her sitting on the grass, grinned, and said, "I've got one for you."

"What?"

"It's an old one."

"Well, what is it?"

"You remember when we were enemies, I used to make up jingles about you?"

"Yeah, I remember."

"Remember the one—

Veronica Ganz
Has ants in her pants?"

Veronica stood up.

"Well, if you were dead, I'd have to change it to—

Veronica Ganz
Had ants in her pants."

Veronica came at him then, and he dodged around a convenient stone and shouted, "Or maybe a better one would be—

She liked plants
Did Veronica Ganz."

"Wait till I get my hands on you," Veronica yelled, but she was laughing too.

They chased each other up and down the path until they saw some grownups in the distance. Then they began walking decorously along, holding their skates behind them. Veronica said, leering at him, "I've got one for you."

"What?"

> "Peter Wedemeyer had a friend
> And that was how he met his end."

And she landed a quick kick on his shins before she got away.

Later, they climbed up to the elevated train platform in their skates and stood hanging over the back railing. They could see beyond the rooftops to where the lights of the city made patterns against the darkening blue sky. They stood there together, quietly looking at the lights until the train pulled into the station.

9

"Where's Rosalie?" Papa said, sitting down at the kitchen table.

Mama put a plate of salad on the table and smiled mysteriously. "You'll see a new girl when she comes home tonight."

Papa put his napkin on his lap. "What do you mean?"

"I gave her the money," said Mama triumphantly, looking at the clock. "'Here,' I said to her, 'I'm treating you. Go get a permanent—one of those new hair styles all the young girls are wearing. Don't be a stick-in-the-mud.' So she listened to me for a change and made an appointment at the beauty parlor for after work, and we'll see."

"Don't send for honey when sugar is sweet," remarked Papa, selecting a pickle and some tomatoes from the platter.

"Tomorrow night," Mama continued, ignoring her

husband's bit of wisdom, "Bernard's taking her to the Knights of Pythias banquet. She'll wear a new dress—I made her buy it—and Tillie's fur coat—I borrowed that—and she'll have a beautiful new hair style, and we'll see, we'll see."

"She looks fine to me," Papa said stubbornly.

"Ma, what's for supper?" Peter asked, without much hope. Tonight being Thursday generally meant fish, and fish was not one of Peter's favorite foods.

"Fish," his mother said, bending down and inspecting the interior of the stove.

"What's for dessert?" Peter continued, a little more hopefully.

"Chocolate pudding."

"So, Peter, how was school today?" his father asked.

"Oh, Pa, you should have seen me today. Both times I was up when we played stickball, I hit a homer. The second time, two men were on base and pow— we won seven to three." Peter chuckled. "You should have seen that ball go."

"Very nice," said his father, "but I meant Hebrew School. Is Rabbi Weiss satisfied with you?"

Mama brought the platter of baked fish and potatoes to the table and began portioning it out.

"Why shouldn't he be satisfied?" she said. "The boy never misses a day. He does all his work. He knows Hebrew better than any other boy in his class. What's for Rabbi Weiss not to be satisfied?"

"I guess he thinks I'm doing O.K.," Peter said. "A little piece, Ma, please, not so much."

His mother finished distributing the food and sat down at the table.

"It's only a month off now," she said thoughtfully. "We'll really have to start getting everything organized. Did you ask the men at the shop—Ralph Spector and Sy Wurtzman and the others to come?"

"Not yet, but I will," Papa said.

"Tell them to bring their families too," Mama said. "I'll have enough for everybody."

Peter nibbled carefully around the exterior of his piece of fish and moved on to the potatoes.

"Are you inviting Rose Lerner?" Papa asked.

"Should I? She didn't invite us to Harriet's wedding."

For months now, his parents had been discussing Peter's bar mitzvah and the party that was to follow. First there would be the services in the synagogue on Saturday morning, when he and one other boy would read portions of the Torah and make their bar-mitzvah speeches. Afterward, all the guests would return to the house to eat, drink, and rejoice. A new, silk-fringed tallith, the traditional prayer shawl worn by men, lay wrapped in tissue paper in a box in his parents' closet. His father had bought it for him, and on the day of his bar mitzvah, would present it to him in the synagogue as a symbol of his arrival at religious maturity under Jewish law.

Only a month away now, and he would be thirteen, no longer a child. On May 27, a Thursday, his birthday would take place, and on the following Saturday, his bar mitzvah.

He had been to many bar mitzvahs of friends and relations in the past. Some of the boys had been nervous, some solemn, some radiant. But one way or another, all had passed their initiation into manhood and had starred in the festivities that followed. There would be gifts too, many gifts, and although Peter tried hard to ignore the worldly part of his bar mitzvah—as Rabbi Weiss urged all his students—and keep his mind solely on the spiritual end of it, still his heart thumped joyfully at the flow of presents that would certainly come.

He was not nervous at all about his performance in the synagogue. He had studied hard, had understood what he was studying, and spoke Hebrew with an ease that delighted his teacher and troubled his fellow students. When the day arrived, he would be ready. That it would be a day filled only with joy, spiritual as well as material, he had no doubt at all.

Listening to his father and mother discussing the guests to be invited reminded him that he had not as yet issued any invitations on his own, so he put his fork down and said, "Ma, can I invite all my friends?"

"Sure," said his mother, smiling. "It's your day—whoever you like. There'll be plenty of everything."

"Knishes?" Peter said hopefully.

"That reminds me," Mama said. "I'm glad you mentioned it. I'll tell Jake to make the little ones. They're fancier. Maybe some with chopped liver too."

She stopped talking suddenly and looked intently at Peter.

"Who are you going to invite?"

"My friends. You just said I could invite anybody I wanted."

"Who?" his mother insisted.

"Well—Marv." His mother nodded. "Bill, Paul—some of the kids in my class."

"And who else?"

Peter looked at her and realized that he might as well get it over with now.

"I'm going to invite her, too, Ma, so just don't say no."

"Invite who?"

"Veronica."

His mother pushed her plate away and stood up. "You are not going to invite that girl! Anybody else you can invite, but that girl is not coming into my house."

Peter stood up and shouted, "If she doesn't come, neither will I. You can have the bar mitzvah without me."

"Jennie!" his father said, warningly, "Sit down, Jennie! Peter, don't you shout at your mother! Sit down! We're civilized people. We'll talk."

"Where does he go with her?" Mrs. Wedemeyer

cried. "A whole day on Sunday, he's gone. Where? What does he do?"

"I told you, I went skating," Peter said between his teeth, but in a lower voice. "I just went skating. What do you think I'm doing—robbing banks?"

"I wouldn't be surprised with a girl like that. But you will not invite her to this house. I can't stop you from seeing her outside, but this is my house, and she is not coming inside as long as I live!"

"Sit down! SIT DOWN!" commanded Papa. Peter and his mother obeyed, but they glared at each other from across the table.

"I know, I know," Mama said angrily, turning suddenly toward her husband. "You're going to take his part. You always take his part."

"No," said Mr. Wedemeyer, "I'm only going to say what's right and that's not taking anybody's part."

Peter also looked at his father, and there was warmth and comfort in that look. It would all come right now that his father had taken over. His father was a man of reason who loved justice, and Peter knew that justice would now prevail. She might yell a little and argue, but she would ultimately, as she had always done in the past, respect her husband's wishes. And what those wishes were, Peter thought he knew very well. For there was only one way for a man who was wise and just to act. He leaned back in his chair and listened.

"Peter," his father said gently, "you must not invite this girl if your mother objects."

"Pa," Peter cried in horror, "how can you say such a thing?"

His mother sighed happily. "You see," she said, "if Papa says so then it must be so."

"Think about it, Peter," his father continued. "What does it mean being bar mitzvahed. What is the party? Nothing. Even the ceremony in the synagogue is not important. What is important is that you're supposed to be a man now, not a child who whines for his own way without understanding the consequences. What does it mean being a man? It means responsibility. And you have a responsibility to respect your parents first and foremost. Not only because it says so in the Bible, but because you're old enough now to realize that your mother has done a great deal for you, more than anybody else in this world, and it's only fair that you respect her wishes in something that matters so much to her. Believe me, Peter, it doesn't make any difference to me whether your friend comes or not. As a matter of fact, if it gave you pleasure, I'd be glad to have her come. But your mother objects. Maybe she's wrong. Maybe not. That's not the point. Whether you agree with her or not, this is her house, and you must not invite this girl if your mother says no."

Peter looked down at his plate and thought to himself, She will come or I won't. But he said nothing.

"If you like, Peter," said his father, "I'll talk this over with Mama and try to persuade her to let your friend come. But if she refuses, then you will have to respect her wishes."

"And she's going to keep on refusing," said his mother happily. "Now let's have some chocolate pudding."

They heard the door open, and Rosalie came into the kitchen. Yesterday her hair had hung very straight, down to her shoulders without a single wave in it. She had worn her hair that way for as long as Peter remembered. But now, from out of the scent of hair lotion, Rosalie stood with her hair in short, tight curls, plastered close to her head.

"Oiy!" said Peter's father in horror.

Rosalie burst into tears and fled.

"What did you have to say 'Oiy' for?" hissed Mama, rising from her seat.

"She looks terrible," whispered Papa. "What did they do to her? She looks like a clown."

"Just don't say 'Oiy,'" said Mama, and she hurried out of the room.

Papa sighed. "Women!" he muttered. "Never satisfied with the way things are. Beauty parlors they call them. They should be called ugly parlors."

"Pa," Peter said slowly, "what you said about being a man, and taking responsibility . . ."

"So?"

"Well, doesn't a man have a responsibility to make fair decisions and do what he thinks is right even if everybody else disagrees?"

"A wise man maketh a glad father
But a foolish man despiseth his mother,"

said Papa kindly. "You've studied the Bible, Peter.
You'll do what's right."

Peter stood up. "I will do what's right," he said.
"And I know it's right to invite Veronica."

"Is it so important to you, Peter, that you would
rather ask this girl, whom you've known only a short
time, than make your mother, whom you've known
all your life, happy? That's not right, is it?"

"But, Papa, it's only because Mama's prejudiced
that she doesn't want me to invite her. It isn't because Veronica's done anything wrong. She's not like
she used to be. Don't you see? It's not fair. It's not
right. It's the principle of the thing."

But his father only shook his head, and Peter ran
out of the kitchen and into his own room, where
even though the door was closed, he could hear
Rosalie's sobs and his mother's voice saying over and
over again, "It'll be all right. It'll be all right."

10

"Are you sure it's all right if I come?" Veronica asked.

"Sure I'm sure," Peter said, even though he wasn't sure at all. With only three weeks to go now, he and his family were still deadlocked over Veronica. He had spoken to Rabbi Weiss, and of course Rabbi Weiss had only said he must respect his parents' wishes. He had drawn Rosalie into the argument, and she had sided with him. But still his mother said no. Every night at his house there were more arguments, more scenes, more tears. The whole atmosphere began to feel more like a funeral, Peter thought, than a bar mitzvah.

So now, on this Friday afternoon, he had just gone ahead and invited her anyway. If his parents persisted in refusing to allow her to come, he had decided that he would ask them to call the whole thing off. But there was no point in going into details with Veronica. She knew how his mother felt about her. He knew how her mother (and Stanley), felt about him. Ever since their conversation on the library steps, it hadn't seemed necessary to discuss family matters any further.

"I mean—nobody'll mind if I come?" Veronica said carefully.

"Look," said Peter, "this is my party, and if I can't invite my friends, then it won't be much of a party. And I especially want you to come. As a matter of fact," Peter clenched his fists, "I want you to come more than anybody else. O.K.?"

"Well, thanks," Veronica said, her face thoughtful. "But what do I do? Where do I go?"

"First you come to the synagogue at nine o'clock in the morning. And then, after the services, you come to my house for the party."

"I've never been inside a synagogue before," Veronica said, twisting up her face. "Stop pulling my hand, Stanley! What do I have to do?"

"Nothing special. Just come and sit down. Oh, wear a hat and maybe a nice dress."

"Like church." Veronica nodded. "But what do I do inside?"

"It's easy. Sit down, and take a prayer book, and just do what everybody else is doing."

"Well, you know, Peter, I'm Lutheran, and I don't know if I'm supposed to do what everybody else is doing in a synagogue."

"Oh, that's right," said Peter. "Well, I guess you

don't have to say or do anything if you don't want
to. Some of the other kids who are coming aren't
Jewish either. Just read the book or look around."

"What do you do?"

"I'm up in the front with the rabbi and the other
boy who's being bar mitzvahed. The two of us read
selections in Hebrew from the Torah—that's the first
five books of the Bible—and then we make speeches."

"In front of everybody?"

"Uh, huh."

"Aren't you scared?"

"Nope." And he wasn't. Not about making the
speech. It was going to be a good one, that he knew.
Most bar-mitzvah speeches dealt with the debt
of gratitude the boy owed to his parents and his
teacher. Peter's speech would also contain the expected words of gratitude, but he had some other
ideas he thought he might also like to include. This
part of his speech he had not discussed with his
teacher, preferring to develop it all by himself. The
idea for it had actually grown out of his friendship
with Veronica, and his struggle in her behalf. He
had some polishing up to do, but by and large, the
speech was completed. He was proud of it and of
himself. It would be somewhat different from other
bar-mitzvah speeches he had heard, somewhat more
important, he thought. Of course, the way matters
stood now, he might never get to give it at all.

"You just be there," he said grimly.

Stanley's skates skidded out from under him and he flopped down on the ground.

On this particular Friday, Stanley had again joined them, on skates, this time, and was occupied at present with clutching Veronica's hands, legs, skirts—whatever he could reach.

Veronica turned her attention to him. "Get up, Stanley, and don't hang on to me. You'll never learn to skate if you hang on."

Stanley remained seated on the ground. "If I don't hold on to you, you'll run away," he said pathetically.

"All right. I promise I won't run away. Now stand up. Here." She held out a hand to him. Stanley grabbed it with both hands and staggered to his feet.

"Now—let go!"

Stanley let go, swayed, skidded, and flopped again to the ground. He began hiccuping.

"Why don't we put him between us," Peter said, "and each of us hold one of his hands. That way we can balance him better."

"I'm not going to hold your hand," Stanley said, turning his special look of loathing on Peter.

"Now look," Veronica said sharply, "nobody wanted you along today, but you said you were just dying to skate. So get up, and you're going to skate whether you like it or not."

She pulled him to his feet, grabbed one hand, and motioned for him to give Peter his other hand. But Stanley's arm hung limply by his side. Peter

put out his hand, took Stanley's, and Stanley clenched
his fist so that Peter ended up holding his thumb.
The three of them began moving along, Veronica
and Peter supporting Stanley between them.

"Who else is going to be there?" Veronica asked,
continuing the conversation.

"Marv, and Paul, and I have to ask Bill, and I
guess some of the girls, and . . ."

"I'm not coming," Stanley said, lurching into Veronica.

"Nobody asked you," Veronica said, yanking him
upright.

Around the corner came Roslyn Gellert and Reba
Fleming. Reba began giggling as soon as she saw
them, and Roslyn seemed to be studying something
in another direction. There was strength in numbers,
and Peter decided that this would be a fine time
to invite Roslyn to his bar mitzvah. And since one
should not harbor thoughts of malice at such an
important occasion, he might as well ask that drip,
Reba, too.

"Hey, Roslyn, Reba," he yelled, letting go of
Stanley's hand and skating in their direction.

Stanley's feet flew out from under him and he fell
down.

"Aw," said Reba, "the poor little kid."

She and Roslyn hurried over and helped Stanley
up.

"Hello, Veronica," Roslyn said. "Is this your
brother?"

"Yeah."

"What a cute little boy!"

Stanley grabbed hold of Roslyn and held on for dear life.

"Roslyn," said Peter, "I'd like you to come to my bar mitzvah. It's three weeks from tomorrow. You too, Reba."

"Thanks," said Reba. "I can come."

Stanley had one arm around Roslyn's neck and the other around her waist.

"There you are, honey," Roslyn cooed. "You won't fall. Just let go of my neck."

"Let go of her neck, Stanley," Veronica ordered.

But Stanley hung paralyzed where he was.

"You're choking me," gasped Roslyn.

Veronica grabbed Stanley and pulled. He hung on. She pulled harder.

"I can't breathe," Roslyn gurgled.

"Let go, Stanley," Peter yelled, and he tried to unfasten Stanley's fingers.

A strong yank from Veronica, and then Stanley came loose, and the two of them were rolling on top of each other on the ground.

"Roslyn," Peter repeated, "I'd like you to come to my bar mitzvah. It's going to be three weeks from tomorrow."

Roslyn's face was very pink. She looked at Stanley and Veronica twisted up together like a pretzel on the ground and suddenly began laughing. Peter followed her gaze. They sure did look funny, wrapped up in each other that way. He began snickering, too, and then Roslyn looked at him, and they smiled at each other, and it was all very comfortable and friendly again.

"I'd love to come Peter. Thanks. I'm sure I can make it."

"Swell," Peter said enthusiastically, and then he added quickly, "How's everything? How are you doing in math?"

"O.K., I guess."

"Well now, don't forget, if you need any help, just ask me."

Roslyn looked away. "Thanks, Peter," she said softly, "I will." She took Reba's arm. "'By now, 'By Veronica, 'By Stanley."

The living knot had disentangled itself and began to assume the vertical. Veronica's face was angry.

"Come on, Stanley, we're going home." She pulled Stanley to his feet and began skating away from Peter.

"Hey, wait," Peter yelled, going after her. "What's wrong?"

"You laughed," Veronica said sullenly.

"Well, so what? You sure looked funny, the two of you."

"If it was you, you wouldn't think it was so funny. I'm going home."

Peter put an arm on Veronica's shoulder. "Don't be like that, Veronica. I'm sorry if I laughed, but— here—this is what you looked like."

He began lurching back and forth, making crazy, clownlike gestures. Finally he let one skate skid and went down, twisting himself up as he went.

Veronica looked down at him coldly.

He crossed his eyes at her.

She pursed up her lips in disdain.

He made Mortimer Snerd noises at her. She blinked. Then he began waggling his tongue and trying to lick his nose. Veronica burst out laughing, and Stanley said sadly, "Aren't we going home, Veronica?"

Peter leaned back on his hands and smiled fondly at Stanley. The kid had his good points after all, and now Roslyn and he were friends again.

"Come on, Stanley, let's skate," said Peter. He stood up, reached for Stanley's thumb where it hung limply at the end of an unresponsive arm, and the three of them were off again.

They came to a big hill, leading down to a busy thoroughfare. He and Veronica had zoomed down it many a time, turning sharply at the end of it to avoid the heavy traffic that always whizzed along the cross street. They stood on the crest, looking down hungrily, and Veronica said, "You sit here, Stanley, and we'll be back up in a second."

"No!" said Stanley.

She took him by both arms and sat him down, protesting, on the pavement.

"Let's go," she cried, and she and Peter flew down the hill with the wind and Stanley's cries spurring them on. At the bottom, each turned sharply in different directions, finding anchorage in the parked cars along the curb.

They climbed back up the hill and Stanley was waiting for them.

"I want to go down too," he said.

"No," said Veronica. "You can't even skate."

"You take me."

"No!"

Stanley hicced, and Peter said generously, grateful for Stanley's presence today, "Look, if I hold him by one hand and you hold him by the other, we can do it."

"No!"

"I wanna go," shouted Stanley. "I wanna go."

He offered his thumb to Peter, and Veronica smiled and said, "Well . . ."

"I wanna go."

"O.K.," said Veronica, "but don't fall."

The three of them stood poised at the top of the hill.

"Get ready," said Peter, "get set."

"Go," shouted Stanley.

And they were off. Peter tried hard to keep a tight grip on Stanley's thumb, but it kept wiggling. Stanley managed to skim along with them though, and at the bottom he yanked his thumb out of Peter's hand. Thinking that Stanley had gone along with Veronica, Peter made his sharp turn, anchored himself around a parked car, and turned, smiling, to look at Veronica

and Stanley. There was only Veronica on the opposite
side of the street, leaning against a parked car and
looking at him in horror.

"Didn't he go with you?" she shouted.

"No—didn't he go with you?"

"Oh—no!"

For a moment he couldn't look. He just couldn't.
All those cars and buses whizzing along, and little
Stanley, poor, little Stanley who couldn't skate, some-
where lost under them.

And then Veronica began screaming, "Stanley!
Stanley! Stanley!"

Peter took a deep, terrified breath and looked. The
cars were still whizzing along, and from across the
broad, busy street, Stanley stood on the sidewalk,
waving and laughing and marvelously safe.

Peter got across first. "Are you all right?" he cried.
"What happened?"

And then Veronica was there. She grabbed Stanley, and pulled him close to her, and said, "Stanley,
Stanley, oh, Stanley!"

"I can skate," Stanley said, pushing her away.
"Now, I can skate. Come on, Peter. Let's do it
again."

He offered Peter his whole hand this time, which
was, in this afternoon of miracles, the greatest miracle
of all.

11

But there was nothing miraculous in the weeks that followed. His mother said no. His father said no. And Peter stubbornly kept insisting that if Veronica didn't come, then he wouldn't either.

He began to dread the evenings after dinner when the family would sit around the kitchen table and begin discussing the bar mitzvah. It would start with his mother wondering how many pickled tongues and corned beefs she should cook, or whether the tailor would finish the alterations on Peter's new suit in time, and why she still hadn't heard from the cousins in New Jersey. His father would talk to him about his studies and listen to him read the portion from the Torah that he would recite during the services. Then the fireworks would begin as he brought up, as he did every night, the issue that was making them all tense and unhappy—Veronica.

Over and over again, back and forth, the arguments

would fly. His mother would cry. His father would point out to him how childishly he was behaving. Rosalie would insist that it was his bar mitzvah and he should invite whomever he wanted. And he would continue to repeat that if she didn't come, then neither would he. He grew exhausted and unhappy at the misery he was bringing down upon his family. But he knew he was right, and the justice of his position burned inside of him.

A few nights before the bar mitzvah, when the arguments had raged fruitlessly all evening, Peter got up from the table, ran into his room, threw himself on his bed, and began crying. After a while, he heard the door open, and somebody came and sat down on the bed and laid a hand on his shoulder.

The hand began slowly patting, and Peter, knowing that it was his mother, lay with his face buried in the bedspread and tried to check his sobs. Then she said, with a sigh, "You're wrong. You'll understand when you grow up that you're wrong." The hand began patting again and then she said, "It means so much to you then?"

"Yes," he cried into the bedspread. "More than anything else."

She took a deep breath, and said, "Come, sit up. We have a lot to do."

He sat up and looked at her, and she took his face in her hands and smiled at it. "Such a face!"

she said, "For a bar mitzvah boy, everything should be golden. Invite the girl then and be happy."

He threw his arms around her neck and kissed her face over and over again, and she said stubbornly, "But you're wrong. You're wrong."

Wrong or right, the next few days were filled for him with excitement and a fierce glory in his triumph.

He spoke to Veronica again in school on Friday. He would not be skating with her that afternoon. He told her to be at the synagogue at nine o'clock in the morning and he urged her not to be late.

Her face had a funny look, but she nodded and said she knew where the synagogue was.

And then it was the day. All the way to the synagogue, his mother brooded. She knew that her honey cakes were not up to her usual mark. She was certain that there would not be enough chairs and not nearly enough food. And she couldn't understand why the cousins from New Jersey had never answered her invitation. His father kept telling her to be calm, and kept telling Rosalie to be calm, and Peter to be calm in a voice that shook with nervousness.

So many people were at the synagogue that morning. Peter tried to keep his mind on his speech as the family took their seats and waited for the services to begin. Across the aisle from where he was sitting, he saw Nathan Katz, the other boy who was also being bar mitzvahed today, move nervously under

his mother's hands as she tugged at his collar and
tie. The funny thing was that he didn't feel at all
nervous. Frozen, maybe, but not nervous. He longed
to turn around in his seat and look at all the people,
but it would not be seemly.

Uncle Irving came up to shake his hand and his
father's hand. His mother wiped her eyes and said,
"If only Papa had lived to see this day!" Peter's
grandfather had died a year ago, but his grandmother, leaning on Uncle Jake's arm, came down
the aisle, kissed Peter, and sat down next to his
mother.

"Did you take the pickled herring out of the
refrigerator?" she whispered.

"Yes. I only hope it's enough."

"It'll be enough. Jake has the knishes in his car.
Did Sadie bring the spongecake last night?"

The services began, and the rustling and fidgeting
settled into attention as the cantor's voice sang the
opening prayers. When the ark was opened and the
Torah brought forth, Peter and Nathan Katz were
called up to the altar to take their place with the
other men around the holy book. His mother gripped
his hand as he rose to go, and he tried to look
calm and untroubled as he walked up the steps to
the pulpit.

When it was his turn to read a portion from the
Torah, he could hear the silence throbbing against
his head. He began to speak, and the Hebrew words
that he had practiced for so long sounded unfamiliar

and very important. He focused all his attention on
the book in front of him, marveling at how the
words flew out in a voice that did not seem to be
his own. But there was no break, no uncertainty,
no stumbling, and when he finished reading and
stole one quick glance toward his mother and saw
her radiant face, he knew that in this, at least, he
had not failed her.

He took a seat in the back of the dais along
with Nathan and his teacher, and waited until he
should be called upon again to make his bar mitzvah
speech.

While the rabbi preached his sermon, he was able
to look over all the faces in the congregation. So
many people—so many cousins and uncles and aunts.
He saw Marv Green, smiling at him, and Reba. He
tried to catch a glimpse of Veronica, wondering
where she was and what she would think of his
speech. But there were so many people that he
couldn't find her.

Nathan Katz spoke first. He thanked his parents,
his teacher, his friends, and relations for helping
him to arrive at this important day. He pledged
himself to be a credit to his family and promised
to carry out the obligations and duties that his
religion required of him. It was a short speech,
spoken with modesty and sincerity. Nathan was a
serious boy and a good student.

Then it was Peter's turn. He walked to the pulpit
and began speaking. He, too, thanked his parents,

his teacher, and the rabbi for their help and support, and he also promised to try to be a credit to them and to the Jewish religion. But then he said, feeling nervous for the first time, "All over the world, people are fighting and killing each other because their hearts are filled with hatred. I pledge myself to work for better understanding among all men so that one day, the word of God as shown to Isaiah will be fulfilled.

"And they shall beat their swords into plowshares
And their spears into pruning hooks
Nation shall not lift up sword against nation
Neither shall they learn war any more."

He finished, shook hands with the rabbi, his teacher, Nathan, sat down again, and saw the rabbi turn to the congregation, sigh, and say, "What generations of wise men have failed to do, this boy hopes to accomplish." There was a ripple of laughter from the congregation, and Peter felt his cheeks grow hot.

But the rabbi continued. "And yet, what would the world be without the vision of the young, the purity of the dreamer? Who knows? Perhaps if the world of tomorrow is filled with people who feel the way Peter Wedemeyer feels, perhaps it will indeed be a better world. We can only hope it will."

Then he went on to congratulate both boys, and

to speak of the excellence of their scholarship and of the fine families that both were lucky to have.

And then it was over. Outside of the synagogue, Peter was passed from hand to hand, kissed, praised, pummeled. His mother said, "Oh, you were wonderful! The best! I never heard anyone in my whole life as good as you!"

And his father shook his hand and said, "Not bad. Not bad at all."

Back at his house, there were tables set up in the living room, heavy with food. There was pickled herring, corned beef, turkey, tongue, platters of potato salad, coleslaw, pickled beets, chick-peas, pickles, and olives. There were bottles of wine, beer, soft drinks, and "schnapps" for the men. There were braided loaves of challah, honey cakes, spongecakes, apple strudel, nutcakes and Uncle Jake's fragrant knishes. There were boxes of candies, nuts, halvah, raisins, and beautiful pyramids of fruit. There was enough, more than enough, in spite of his mother's fears.

Peter stood at the door greeting the guests as they came, thanking them for their good wishes and the myriad of presents that were heaped upon him. Rosalie kept carrying armloads of boxes into another room, and it seemed a miracle that so many people were able to fit into one small apartment.

"You look like a stuffed turkey," Bill whispered in his ear as he handed him a small, flat package.

Roslyn shook his hand and said seriously, "I liked

your speech. That was wonderful what you said. Everybody thought you were so good."

And Reba giggled.

All the kids crowded around him, and his mother, her face glowing, came over and said, "Come, come, everybody! Help yourself. Peter, go take Grandma a glass of wine. Come on, everybody. Rosalie—where's Rosalie—go get some more napkins, Rosalie."

Bustling, and urging everybody to eat, she moved happily all over the room. It was her day, too, and Peter felt a great easing inside of him. It was all over then, all but the pleasure. The work, the worries, the arguments—nothing remained now but the clink of glasses, the laughter, and the rejoicing.

And where was Veronica? Although he knew his mother would never be rude to a guest in her own house, still and all it was too much to expect her to lavish any particularly warm welcome on the one person who had threatened to disrupt the whole day. He would personally guide Veronica over to the food-laden tables, heap up a plate of goodies for her, and perhaps, listen to what she had to say about his speech. She, of all people, would know that his speech was built around their friendship. She, more than anybody else, would be able to appreciate what he had said. He had written the last part of his speech with her in mind. That whole bit about "working for better understanding among all men" was directly related to all the problems he had encountered just because he had made a friend with somebody "different." Veronica would understand what he meant. Veronica would know he was thinking of her. Veronica would be grateful.

He brought his grandmother a glass of wine, and then his father introduced him to some of the men at the shop where he worked. Uncle Irving talked to him for a while about what had happened at his bar mitzvah in the old country. Other relatives spoke to him, and it seemed like ages had passed before he was free to look around for Veronica again.

She was nowhere in the house. He had a dreadful vision of her waiting shyly outside and hurried into the hall and out onto the stoop.

Some of his younger cousins had carried their plates of food outside and were sitting on the steps picnicking.

"Hey, Peter," his cousin, Aaron, called, "did you see what I brought you?"

"No, not yet," Peter said, looking up the street in dismay. She was nowhere in sight. Could she have come then, while he was busy talking, waited around for him to notice her, and left, feeling ignored and unwelcome? Oh, no! He hurried back into the apartment and bumped into Marv, who was coming through the door carrying a plate filled with food.

"Your mother's so nice," Marv said happily. "She wants me to take this to my father since he couldn't come."

"Say, Marv," Peter said quickly, "did you see Veronica?"

"No," said Marv, moving out the door. "I'll be right back."

Peter hurried back into the apartment and looked carefully into all the groups and subgroups standing around. She was not there. Then where was she? Had she come and left? Had she come at all?

Looking through the closest knot of people, he saw Bill raising a Coke to his lips and called out to him, "Bill, come here a second, will you."

Bill gurgled a little, but obligingly threaded his way through the crowd. "It's a great party, Peter," he said approvingly. "Your mother's some cook!"

"Thanks," Peter said quickly. "Listen, did you see Veronica?"

Bill stiffened. "Is *she* coming?"

"Did you see her at the synagogue?" Peter asked, tensing.

"No, I didn't."

"Peter," his father called, coming up to him, "come here. I want you to meet Mr. Stein. He's the one whose boy is studying to be a rabbi. They're both over near the window."

He took Peter's arm and began pulling him through the crowd.

"Oh, Pa," Peter whispered, "Pa!"

"What?"

"Pa. She didn't come."

"Who didn't come?"

He turned a sick, empty face up to his father, and when his father saw Peter's face, he gripped his arm tighter and looked around for a place to go. The only empty place was the bathroom, and his father led him there, locking the door behind him.

"What is it, Peter? What's wrong?"

"She didn't come."

"That girl, you mean?"

Peter nodded, and his misery was greater than anything he had felt before.

"Are you sure?"

"I'm sure."

"So it was for nothing then," his father said kindly. "My poor boy!" He put an arm on Peter's shoulder and murmured, "Beware of your friends, not your enemies."

"She's not my friend any more," Peter said bitterly.

His father smoothed his hair and straightened his tie. "Come now," he said gently. "No more today. People are waiting for you. Don't disappoint them."

Peter nodded, followed his father out of the room, and did what was expected of him. But it stayed, drumming in his head the rest of the day. Over and over again it said, "She didn't come. She didn't come. She didn't come."

12

Peter was busy examining the Bible Aunt Sadie and Uncle Lester had given him. It was Sunday morning, and he had spent the last couple of hours poring over the presents he had received. As he had expected, there were numerous fountain pens—enough he speculated to last him through high school. And if you figured the mortality rate for fountain pens at two or three a year, that would still leave quite a margin for college and perhaps several to see him into adulthood. That old joke about the bar-mitzvah boy saying, "Today I am a fountain pen," wasn't such a joke after all.

With quite a number of packages still to go, Peter had unwrapped three sweaters, nine ties, five tie clips, two bathrobes, a chemistry set, a dictionary and a number of other books dealing with assorted Jewish subjects, stationery, a handsome leather brief case, a subscription to *National Geographic Magazine*,

an ivory colored chess set, a globe of the world, and
a new stamp album from Bernard.

The Bible, which he was admiring at the moment,
had a white leather cover into which THE BIBLE,
and lower down, PETER WEDEMEYER—1941 had
been tooled in gold. It was very impressive, and
Peter was just beginning to think about looking inside of it when Rosalie came in from outside.

She was carrying the Sunday paper, and stood for
a moment contemplating the pool of presents Peter
was submerged in.

"Wow!" she said, "what a haul."

"Look at this, Rosalie," Peter said, holding up the
Bible.

"It's gorgeous," Rosalie said. "You'll have to take
good care of it and see that your hands are clean
before you handle it."

"Aw, Rosalie, cut it out!" Peter said impatiently.

"What's that, over there?" Rosalie asked, pointing
to the stamp album.

Peter picked it up and handed it to her. He had
an idea she knew who it was from. "Bernard gave
it to me," he said, trying to sound enthusiastic, even
though it was not exactly the one he would have
chosen. "It's a very nice one."

"Bernard knows what to buy," Rosalie said approvingly, flipping through the pages.

Peter looked up at her. Her short curls still stood
out in different directions on her head, but her face
looked happy.

"He thinks a lot of you," she said.

"That's nice," Peter said politely. "He's a pretty nice fellow himself."

"I'm glad you like him," Rosalie said, looking very happy. Then she said quickly, "Oh, I was forgetting —your friend is downstairs, Peter. She was standing there in front of the house when I went down for the paper. I asked her to come up, but she said she'd wait for you to come down."

Veronica's betrayal had been nagging at Peter all morning. It had woken up along with him, nudged him like a poke in the stomach all through breakfast, and it was only under the weight of all the un-wrapped presents, that it had temporarily been buried. It started up again at Rosalie's words.

"Let her wait," Peter said bitterly.

"Well, I said I'd tell you," Rosalie said vaguely, "and, Peter, you will remember to thank Bernard for the album, won't you?"

"No, I'll kick him in the shins," Peter said angrily. "You don't have to tell me that. Don't you think I know?"

"O.K., O.K., cookie," Rosalie said soothingly. She shifted the paper to her other arm, smiled at Peter, snuck a kiss in on his cheek, and walked out of the room.

Let her wait, Peter thought, but he put down the Bible and stood up. No. He'd go down and tell her off. He'd feel a lot better once he told her off. And boy, would he tell her off!

He hurried through the apartment, out the door, and through the vestibule. The force of his speed whipped his anger up to a fury, and when he flew through the outer door, onto the stoop, and saw Veronica standing a little distance away from the house, his face felt as if it was on fire.

"What do you want?" he shouted.

"Hi, Peter," Veronica said, a weak smile on her face. She walked slowly toward him, and before he could say anything else, she held out a package. "Here, it's for you. I've been waiting for you so I could give it to you."

He took it and held it and just looked at her, and it was like he was seeing her for the first time. How big she was! He'd always known she was big, bigger than anyone else, and it had always seemed to him in the past, a fine thing being big. But she was too big, he saw that now, big and clumsy, and just look at her clothes! The buttons were off her jacket. There was a safety pin where the top button should have been, and her slip stuck out from beneath her skirt, and her socks wrinkled and flopped around her ankles. Slowly and piercingly, his eyes traveled up and down the whole messy, clumsy hulk of Veronica Ganz. No wonder the other kids didn't bother with her. No wonder they laughed at her. Sure—they'd been laughing at him, too, and boy, he'd had it coming. His mother had been right. What could he possibly have in common with a girl like her, a girl whom nobody liked, a girl who had no friends, a girl who didn't know what it meant to be a friend.

"Aren't you going to open it, Peter?" she said.

He tore open the package, and inside lay a pair of green cuff links. Just what he needed, he thought angrily—cuff links! He didn't have a single shirt that required cuff links. She just couldn't do anything right.

"They're emerald cuff links," Veronica said, "because your birthday's in May, and emerald is the birthstone for May, so I thought . . ."

"Thanks," Peter said, interrupting her, "thanks a lot." He tossed the box on the ledge and continued glaring at her.

"Was it . . . was it nice yesterday?" Veronica asked, shifting uneasily under his stare.

"Just great!"

"Look, Peter," Veronica moved a little closer to him. "I think you're angry at me, but . . ."

"Angry!" Peter laughed. "Why should I be angry at you? I just fought with everybody in my family, and made a jerk out of myself, and made everybody miserable so that you could come to my bar mitzvah. But no—you couldn't take the trouble to come after all I went through. But that's O.K.," he said quickly. "You just didn't care, and that's all right with me."

"Peter," Veronica cried, "I didn't know."

"You didn't know," he hissed at her, sticking his neck, snakelike, all the way out at her. "I asked you over and over again to come. I didn't have to spell

it out for you. You knew what I was up against.
Don't tell me you didn't know."

"But I didn't, Peter. I didn't." Veronica's face was
tight and unhappy. "Sure I knew your mother didn't
like me. I figured she'd just as soon I didn't come,
and I thought maybe it would be easier for you if
I didn't. Honestly, I swear to God, I didn't know
you were having all that trouble. If I had, Peter,
I swear to you, Peter . . ."

"You still wouldn't have come," Peter shouted. "You
know you wouldn't have. Like you didn't come to
Lorraine's party. You said you were coming, and I
had a fight with Bill because of you, and Roslyn—
well, never mind about that—but because of you
I had a lousy time at that party, and because of you
my whole bar mitzvah was ruined. I was ready to
give up even having the bar mitzvah if you couldn't
come. For weeks my whole family fought and was
miserable until I got them to say you could come.
But that's O.K. I learned the kind of friend you are,
and now I'm finished.

Veronica said slowly, "Peter, you're my best
friend, and I'd do anything for you . . ."

"Yeah," he taunted, "I know, I know. If I was
dead, you'd plant rosebushes, and tell everybody how
smart I was, and about the white stripe I had down
my back. Ha, ha," Peter began laughing. "What a
joke! Wait'll I tell the other kids—boy, will they
laugh. You're a good friend to have if you're going

to die, but when you plan on living, you're not worth much, Veronica Ganz."

Veronica's face was white. She clenched her fists when Peter began to laugh, and he moved a little nervously away from her.

"Don't do that," she cried. "Not even you, Peter. I can't stand it. Don't laugh at me. Don't make fun of me."

"Just go away then," Peter said, and his legs began trembling under him, not from fear, but from exhaustion. "Go away! Go away!"

Veronica began talking very quickly. "I didn't know. That's true. And if you'd told me, I would have come because you wanted me to come. I don't like parties. I don't like to go places where there are lots of people. I feel funny and scared. That's why I didn't go to Lorraine's party. I was all dressed and ready to go, and I got scared. And yesterday, I was all ready to go to your bar mitzvah, and don't think that my mother was happy about me going either. But I was going to go, and I looked at myself in the mirror and I got scared. But I didn't know that it would matter so much to you, and if I had, even though I was scared, I'd have come."

Peter's legs buckled, and he sat down on the stoop and tried to sound unconcerned when he said, "Who cares anyway? It's over and done with."

"That's right," Veronica said eagerly. "It is over and done with. Let's forget about it. I'm sorry, Peter, I'm really sorry. You're right. Let's forget about it.

Come on, get your skates. We'll go skating. We won't even talk about it any more."

"I'm busy," Peter said, looking away.

"Well then, Friday, O.K.?" She laughed quickly. "I'll make sure Stanley doesn't come."

"I'll be busy Friday," he said stubbornly.

She stood over him, and he kept his eyes focused on her feet. Her socks didn't match. One had ribbing and one didn't. He concentrated on the one that didn't have ribbing and began thinking about it. Was it a white sock that had yellowed, or was it a yellow sock that had faded? It seemed important to come to some conclusion about it, and he kept his eyes on it until suddenly, it wasn't there any more.

When he stood up, she was halfway up the block, and he waited for her to turn around. But she didn't. So after a while, he walked back through the vestibule door, and then he remembered and returned to the stoop. The box was still there, so he picked it up, hurried inside, and dropped it on his desk. But later in the day, when he was sated and nearly happy again after re-examining all his gifts, he saw it there, and opened it, and looked with disdain at the cheap, dime-store cuff links with their garish, green stones. And he took up the box, and ran into the kitchen, and threw it in the garbage can.

13

It was Stanley who started him thinking about her again, and Marv who made him feel so rotten.

All those weeks, he'd hardly given her a thought. For a week or so after the bar mitzvah, he'd still felt angry and purposely avoided her. He began walking to school with the other kids, watching her lumbering along in the distance, alone, as she deserved to be. But school had ended in June, and there had been plenty to do, what with playing ball with the other kids, swimming, reading, and working on the moat with Marv. He'd almost forgotten about her, and when he did think about her it was with irritation and relief that no longer did he have to fight off the whole world over her. She just had not been worth all that trouble. Thank goodness it was over.

Now, in mid-August, with the summer at its peak, and with one easy day like another, with nothing that you had to do—no homework, no Hebrew School —only ices to eat, and mosquito bites to scratch, and endless, hot, languorous days to float through, he was beginning to feel just a little restless, just a little excited about the prospect of school starting up again, and a little hungry for the sound of the alarm clock in his sleepy ears. Just a little.

A stubborn crack had developed in one wall of the moat late in July, and the water continually seeped out. He and Marv had been working away patiently, tracking the crack to its source, cementing, exulting, despairing, and facing failure at every turn. The water would not stay in. Today they would try again, but first he had to go to the egg store and buy a dozen cracked eggs for his mother. Heat or no, she had determined to make a spongecake. Bernard was expected for dinner tonight, and lately his mother had been throwing all her talents into preparing the most exquisite dishes for him. Rosalie's hair had grown in and her face had become increasingly happy. His mother seemed to feel that the situation was close to a crisis, and that her contribution in bringing matters to a productive conclusion lay in the state of Bernard's stomach.

Peter bought the eggs and was on his way home again, when along came Stanley.

"Hey, Peter," Stanley yelled. "Hello, Peter."

Stanley seemed happy to see him, and Peter looked around uncomfortably to see if Veronica was some-

where about too. Come to think of it, he hadn't
seen her far or near for quite awhile.

But Stanley was alone. He hurried up to Peter,
and pulled a letter out of his pocket, and waved it
proudly. "I got another letter today. And yesterday,
I got a post card. She only wrote a couple of times
to my mama, but she writes all the time to me."
Stanley's bright face suddenly dimmed. A look of
suspicion spread across it. "How many times did she
write to you?"

"Who?" asked Peter.

"Her! Veronica!"

"Well, where is she?" Peter said impatiently.

"You know," Stanley insisted. "She's visiting her
papa. She and Mary Rose. They went with their
Uncle Charles all the way on the train. They slept
on the train, and they ate on the train, and she sent
me a picture post card of the train."

"I didn't even know she was away," Peter said,
feeling strangely irritated that she should be enjoying such an adventure without his even hearing
about it. Of course, he knew her father lived in Las
Vegas, and that Veronica and her sister hadn't seen
him since they were babies. What had happened
suddenly to bring about their going? He had a sudden righteous feeling that it was his mediation between her and her uncle that had brought about the
trip.

Grumpily, he questioned Stanley. "When did she
go?"

"Right after school ended."

"When is she coming back?"

"Soon." Stanley's face looked suddenly drawn. "They didn't tell me she was going to go. My papa took me to the zoo that day, and I ate hot dogs and popcorn and three root beers, and when I came home, she was gone, and Mary Rose too." Stanley began hiccuping. "So my mama said I could sleep in their bed that night, and my papa bought me a wagon the next day, and she sent me an Indian belt, and lots of post cards and letters, and . . ."

Stanley stopped talking and stood there hiccing, with such an abandoned look in his eyes that even Peter was moved to pat him gently on the shoulder and say kindly, "Well, I guess she'll be back real soon. School will be starting in a couple of weeks."

"Yeah," Stanley said, happy again. "She's not going to stay there. She's coming home on the train. She said so in her letter. She said she was bringing me a surprise. What do you think she's bringing me?"

"Something nice," Peter said softly. He shifted the eggs and said, "Well, I've got to go now."

"Where?" Stanley asked.

"Home."

"Can I come too?"

"Well, gee, I don't know. Doesn't your mother want you home?"

"She said I could play outside for a while. Can I come with you?"

Stanley followed him into the kitchen. Peter put

the eggs on the table and called into the interior
of the apartment, "Ma, the eggs are on the table."

"Fine," came his mother's voice.

"I'm going now."

"Where are you going?"

"To Marv's."

"Don't get dirty."

"O.K., Ma." With Stanley trotting along at his
heels, he hurried down the stairs, grateful that it
hadn't been necessary to introduce Stanley to his
mother and answer any uncomfortable questions.

Across the street, Marv was already at work, and
a number of neighborhood kids, hopefully clad in
bathing suits, were standing around watching him
and waiting.

"How's it going?" Peter asked.

Marv looked happy. "I think I've got it. Look—
down in that corner. You see where the wall bulges
out? We didn't notice that little hole there, right
under the bulge. I think that's where all the trouble
is coming from."

"Can I take off my shoes?" Stanley said, looking
hungrily into the moat.

"I guess so," Peter said.

"Who's the kid?" asked Marv, looking up.

"Stanley—uh—Veronica's kid brother."

"Oh. Hi, Stanley," Marv said, smiling, and resumed his examination of the wall. Stanley took off
his shoes and socks and jumped down into the moat.
He wasn't hiccuping any more, and after a while, he

climbed out of the moat, crossed over the bridge, and wandered off into the cellar.

"We'll stuff it up with gravel," Marv decided, presenting his diagnosis, "and then cement it over."

"We gonna swim today?" asked one of the neighborhood children.

"Are you gonna fill it up with water soon?" asked another.

"Not today," Marv said pleasantly. "We've got to wait until the cement dries. Maybe in a few days you'll be able to swim."

Some of the children wandered off. A few others joined Stanley in the basement. Throughout the whole summer, the neighborhood children seemed to converge on Marv's house, poking around the moat, playing in the cellar or out in the back yard, where Marv's finished and unfinished structures provided a play area unmatched by any of the city playgrounds. Marv never seemed to mind having younger kids around, and Peter looked thoughtfully toward the cellar where Stanley had gone, and suddenly felt like talking.

"Marv," he said, "could I tell you something?"

"Sure," said Marv, bending over the moat again, his hands probing and exploring like a surgeon's.

"You know Veronica and I aren't friends any more, but I never told you why."

"I figured you had a fight or something," Marv said, climbing down into the moat and bending down to peer into the diseased spot in the wall.

"Do you want to know what really happened?"

"O.K." Marv's hands began patting the area around the hole.

So Peter told him. And all the old anger and hurt came back as he spoke, and he was surprised because he thought it was all over with. He told Marv about his mother's dislike for Veronica, her prejudice, his father's abandonment, and of the whole unhappy, painful time that led up to his bar mitzvah.

Marv nodded as he spoke and said "Oh," and "Gee," and continued working on the hole.

Then Peter said that as bad as all that had been, it was nothing compared to how Veronica had acted, how she had betrayed him, and made his long struggle all for nothing.

"What did she do?" Marv asked, still intent on his work.

"She didn't come." Peter stopped and waited for Marv to react.

"Yeah?" said Marv. "And then what?"

"She just didn't come. She just never showed up."

Marv stopped working and looked at him. "Why not?" he said. "Why didn't she come?"

"Oh, she said she was scared. She said she hated parties. They made her scared. But she just didn't care. That's why she didn't come. Some friend she turned out to be. She couldn't take the trouble to come after all the trouble I went through to get my folks to say she could come," Peter said bitterly, and again waited for Marv to react.

Marv said slowly, "Maybe she *was* scared."

"But that's not the point. Don't you see, if she was really a good friend, she would have come. Why should anybody be scared of parties anyway?"

"I don't know," Marv said, "but maybe she was."

"Don't you get the point?" Peter insisted. "She had to come because of all the trouble I went through to get my parents to let her come. Don't you see?"

Marv blinked but he didn't say anything. He turned his attention back to the hole. That was one thing about Marv. You could never get him to argue. In that respect, he was a lot like his mother.

"Don't you see?" Peter repeated. "She just was a lousy friend."

Marv kept working.

"Marv?" Peter cried.

Marv turned around, looked at Peter, and then looked away. "I think we're going to need more cement," he said unhappily. "I better mix up some more."

He climbed out of the moat and escaped into the cellar. And it was suddenly very clear in Peter's mind what Marv thought and what he was not willing to say.

He sat down on the edge of the moat and knew with certainty that Marv thought *he* had been wrong, and that Veronica had not done anything so terrible after all. She was big and clumsy and scared of parties. And if you have a friend who is big and clumsy and scared of parties, then if you're a good

friend, you just have to like it or lump it. And he
had done neither.

Peter groaned. It was a long summer, and he was
growing tired of doing the same things day after day.
If Veronica was in the city, maybe he'd go back
with Stanley and try to make it up. He'd say, "Let's
forget about what happened. You're the way you are,
and that's all there is to it. Maybe I was wrong to
get so mad, but we'll forget about it now. So get
your skates and let's go."

But she wasn't in the city. Too bad! He felt suddenly overflowing with generosity and pity. Poor big
old Veronica. Let the other kids laugh at her, and
him too. He wasn't going to bear any grudges. He'd
tell her when she returned that he wasn't angry
any more. He'd make it up, and they'd resume where
they left off.

It was good not feeling angry any more. There
were too many more important things to be angry
about. Good old Marv—you could learn something
from anyone. Peter almost chuckled out loud. Marv
was right. He hadn't said anything, but his look had
spoken for him. You take your friends for better or
worse, Marv's look said, and if they were a little bit
different from other kids, why you just try to over-
look those differences. Who knows? Maybe he could
even help her to be more comfortable with the other
kids. Maybe he could try to draw her into the crowd,
get them to like her a little more, suggest some ways
that she could improve herself. Oh, there was a lot

he could, and should do for her. After all, what's
a friend for? And besides, she had her good points
even as she was. A sharp flow of memories suddenly brought back to him the tang of the wind and
the feel of the ground beneath his skates.

He'd make up with her on the first day of school,
and the only regret he had at the moment was that
she wasn't around. Because he could hardly wait to
see her face when he told her that he wasn't angry
with her any more.

14

"Wow!" said Frank, as they were walking through the hall to their English class. "Did you see Veronica?"

"I nearly fell over when I did," Paul said.

And even Bill forgot to make one of his usual wisecracks about her.

Peter felt confused. He'd made up his mind to speak to Veronica on the first day of school. He'd looked for her as he was walking across the park, but she hadn't been in sight. It was only when they were in their new classroom, and Veronica walked through the door, that he'd seen her for the first time since school ended.

She was not the same person. Her hair was cut short, her skin was very tanned, and her eyes seemed much bluer than he had remembered. She was also wearing a pink sweater and skirt that fit her just right. Pink! Veronica Ganz wearing pink, like any other girl. And that's what she looked like—like any other girl.

The only thing that was the same was the way she sat down without looking at anybody, that familiar tight, uncomfortable look on her face. But even that changed. At lunch time, as he was looking at her from across the yard, all by herself, and wondering if he might now go over and talk to her, he saw Lorraine Jacobs approach the bench where she was sitting and stop to talk to her. The next thing he knew, Lorraine was sitting next to her, and after a while, several other girls were parked around them too.

The next morning, she was walking to school with the girls. And the next morning too.

Veronica Ganz was a different person, and yet, after a few days of commenting on the change, everything seemed to settle down, and none of the other kids seemed to remember what she used to be like. It was as if she had always been the way she now was. And when, on Thursday, he saw her and Bill laughing together in the hall, and he turned around to see if anybody else shared his astonishment, nobody even seemed to notice.

What to do then? He tried to smile at her, to catch her eye, to find an opportunity to speak to her alone. But she stubbornly refused to look at him. He thought of going over to her house but for one reason or another kept putting it off. But today was Friday, and Friday had always been special for

the two of them. He made up his mind that if he
didn't get to talk to her in school today, then afterward, he would go over to her house and speak
with her then.

But he had an uncomfortable feeling that the situation had grown much more complicated. Take the
way she was suddenly getting along so well with the
other kids. Wasn't that what he hoped would happen? What he had planned on helping her to achieve?
So why should he feel so rotten when he saw her
laughing and talking with everybody else? He tried
to convince himself that it was only because the
two of them still hadn't made up, and once they had,
why it would even be better than it used to be.
Wasn't it a good thing that she looked so well and
had suddenly become a part of the crowd? He certainly wouldn't want her to go back looking the way
she used to, and talking to nobody but himself. He
wouldn't want that. What kind of a person would
he be if he did?

Well, today he'd just go and straighten it all out.
Tell her he wasn't sore any more, and—then what?
He wasn't quite sure—the way she'd gone and
changed. It was unsettling.

But he did not have to go to her house after all,
because Veronica sought him out. She was waiting
for him Friday morning right in front of his house.
He saw her as he came through the door, and
greeted her with enthusiasm.

"Oh, Veronica! Gee, I'm glad to see you. I was

going to come to your house this afternoon. I've got to talk to you."

"I want to talk to you too," she said, her blue eyes frosty. "That's why I'm here. Let's walk to school on Third Avenue so we can talk without interruption."

"Great," Peter said eagerly. "I've got a lot to say to you."

He began walking next to her and stole a quick look at her face. With satisfaction, he noted that her tan was beginning to fade, although she still looked unnaturally well. No buttons were off her red sweater and her blue plaid skirt hung in crisp, tight pleats. Even her socks matched. Uncomfortably he wondered how he should begin. But she didn't give him a chance.

"I wanted to talk to you," she said, not looking at him, "because I have several things that are on my mind and I want you to know what they are." Her voice was cold, and she spoke in a flat, rehearsed manner, as if she'd practiced saying this before.

"The last time I spoke to you," she continued, "I apologized for not coming to your bar mitzvah."

"Aw, Veronica," Peter interrupted, "let's forget all about that. I was going to tell you . . ."

"Just a minute," she said peremptorily. "Let me finish and then you can say what you like."

Peter nodded unhappily. The conversation was not going in the direction he had planned.

"Now then," she went on, in the same cold, flat voice, "as I said before, last time I saw you I apologized. What I want to do now is to tell you that I am only sorry about one thing, and that is that I did apologize."

She turned to look at him then and her eyes were blazing. "I didn't owe you an apology. You owed me one. I wasn't the bad friend. You were! I never asked you to go and fight with your family over me. I didn't even know you were doing it. And if you had asked me, I would have told you not to, because I didn't want to come to your bar mitzvah. I hate parties. I hate going places where I don't know anybody. And if you were a good friend, you would have thought about my feelings and not your own. And I want to tell you something else—maybe you thought you were such a big hero, fighting against prejudice and all that, but you didn't do anything for me! You didn't even care about me! You didn't even think about me!"

"How can you say that?" Peter yelled, angry and hurt too. "How can you say I didn't care about you, when I wouldn't let my family discriminate against you. I was even willing to give up having the bar mitzvah if they didn't let you come. So how can you say I wasn't thinking about you? Who was I thinking about if I wasn't thinking about you?"

"You!" Veronica cried. "You were thinking about you! About what a great guy you were! It had nothing at all to do with me. Because what did I care if you fought with your family. I didn't ask you to. I didn't want to come. You can't fight for people if they don't want you to fight for them. You've got to see what they want, and all I wanted from you was . . ." Veronica's lips began trembling, and she had to swallow hard a couple of times before she could finish what she was saying. " . . . was for you to be my friend, and it didn't matter a bit to me what your mother said, or what my mother said, or what anybody else said. But you—just because I didn't come to your bar mitzvah—you made fun of me, and stopped being my friend. For a little thing like that. That's all the friendship meant to you.

"So," Veronica continued, catching her breath, and her voice resumed its flat, studied air, "I wanted you to know that if I ruined your bar mitzvah, as you said I did last time we spoke, you have ruined my summer, and more than that, you have destroyed my confidence in friendship. That's all I have to say to you except that I withdraw my apology and hope that I never have to speak to you as long as I live."

"O.K., O.K.," Peter snapped, "now you made your little speech, suppose I make mine."

"There's nothing that you can possibly say," Veronica said loftily, that cool, impassive look again in her eyes, "that would make a bit of difference. I've thought about you all summer, and I know now that you were the worst friend that anybody ever had."

There was a well of words in Peter's throat, but he couldn't speak them. Words he had thought he

would say to her before she'd spoken. Words he
knew now no longer had any meaning. How could
he tell her he wasn't angry any more when she was
so angry? How could he tell her he'd forget and
forgive when she would not?

He looked at the gleaming row of brass buttons
on her sweater and said petulantly, "Don't tell me
I ruined your summer. You don't look like anybody
ruined your summer."

Veronica said, "If you mean because I've got all
these new clothes, that has nothing to do with you.
My father's wife happens to be a saleslady in a de-
partment store in Las Vegas, and before we left, she
got Mary Rose and me a lot of clothes half price."

"Well," Peter said accusingly, "you don't even look
like you any more. I don't know what happened to
you this summer but you just don't look like you."

"I do so look like me," Veronica snapped. "I got
a haircut, that's all. But I don't see what that has
to do with the price of onions. Here I get to go
someplace I've never been in my whole life, to see
my father again and his wife, and everybody's great,
and they do all these great things for us, and take us
all over the place, and what do I keep thinking
about? You! I couldn't enjoy anything because I
kept thinking about all the things I should have said
to you, the way I should have told you off instead
of apologizing like a dope. Ooh!"

She ground her teeth and her eyes began blazing
again.

"You know," Peter said helplessly, "I was really planning on making up with you before I saw you again. Before you showed up looking like, well, not looking like you."

"I do so look like me," Veronica cried.

"Well, anyway," Peter said quickly, "that's not important anyway. You can't help looking the way you look and that's not what I mean. What I mean is . . ." And he stopped, because it came to him then, what he did mean, and he said slowly, "What I really mean is—you're right—and I'm sorry. I guess I got mixed up. I thought because I was sticking my neck out and making a big fuss, you just had to go along with it. But I should have asked you first. Maybe you would have said not to, and maybe I would have anyway, but I had no right blaming you for not going along with me. You're you and I'm me, and I'll try not to forget it, ever again."

She sniffed and looked away from him. They continued walking along together silently until Peter said, "Do you remember, Veronica, the last time I apologized to you?"

"I remember," she said crisply.

"That was after I had gotten the other boys to beat you up, and I felt so bad I just couldn't think about anything else. But do you remember what happened after I apologized?"

"No."

"Sure you do," Peter urged softly. "We became

friends. So now let's do it again. I apologize and let's be friends."

"No!" Veronica said. "That time, maybe I was wrong, too, but not this time. This time, I know what kind of a person you are, and how little friendship means to you. I don't want you for a friend."

"People change," Peter said. "You did, this summer, and it's not only because you got a haircut and new clothes. You changed. How do you know I didn't. If you're the good friend you say you are, how about giving me a chance?"

Veronica did not reply, and the two of them continued walking along slowly.

"I thought maybe we could go skating this afternoon," Peter said enticingly.

"I'm giving my skates away. I'm never skating any more. I'm too old. And besides, Lorraine asked me to come over to her house today so maybe I will."

That there would be complications in the form of Lorraine and other girls, and that Veronica could no longer be considered his exclusive property gave Peter an unpleasant jolt. But there it was and he wasn't going to waste time brooding over it now. So he continued as if she had not spoken. "I thought maybe we could go see my Uncle Jake and get a couple of knishes."

No response from Veronica.

"Or maybe skate down to your uncle's."

No answer.

"Or over to the river."

Veronica tossed her head.

"Or maybe," and Peter played his last trump card lovingly, "we could go over to the cemetery and work a little over Martin Franklin's grave."

"I've been there already."

"You've been there?" Peter said, very hurt. "Without me?"

"Well, I didn't think it mattered to you any more," Veronica said defensively. "I didn't think you cared where I went or what I did."

He stopped walking and she did too. The two of them stood looking at each other. Now the top of his head came up to her nose instead of her chin, as it had formerly, and he didn't have to tilt his head back quite so far to look up at her face.

"I never thought," she said finally, "that it would hurt so much."

"What?" said Peter.

"Having a friend." Veronica's face was perplexed. "Before, maybe I was lonesome sometimes but I don't think I ever felt so bad."

"Well," said Peter happily, measuring the distance from her nose to the top of her head and wondering how long it would take before the top of his own head caught up with hers, "I guess we both have lots of miserable years in store."

She didn't answer him then, but by the time they reached school there was no question in either of their minds about what they would be doing that afternoon.

About the Author

Marilyn Sachs, a native of New York City, received a Bachelor of Arts degree from Hunter College and a master's degree in library science from Columbia University. She has worked in the Brooklyn Public Library as a specialist in children's literature, and in the San Francisco Public Library. The author of over twenty-two books for young readers, she is well known for such distinguished titles as *The Bear's House,* a 1971 nominee for the National Book Award, and *Veronica Ganz,* an ALA Notable Book.

Ms. Sachs now lives with her family in San Francisco.